Frank Richard Stockton

A Borrowed Month and Other Stories

Frank Richard Stockton

A Borrowed Month and Other Stories

ISBN/EAN: 9783744748117

Printed in Europe, USA, Canada, Australia, Japan

Cover: Foto ©Andreas Hilbeck / pixelio.de

More available books at **www.hansebooks.com**

A BORROWED MONTH

AND

OTHER STORIES

BY

FRANK R STOCKTON

Author's Edition

.

EDINBURGH

DAVID DOUGLAS, CASTLE STREET

1887

Frederic Ernest Allsopp.

CONTENTS.

	PAGE
A BORROWED MONTH, ...	9
A TALE OF NEGATIVE GRAVITY, . .	75
THE CHRISTMAS WRECK, ...	119
OUR ARCHERY CLUB, ...	149
A STORY OF ASSISTED FATE, . . .	179
THE DISCOURAGER OF HESITANCY, . .	237
OUR STORY, ...	251

A BORROWED MONTH.

A BORROWED MONTH.

EAST.

ALL persons who, like myself, are artists, and all others who delight in the beauties of lake and valley, the grandeur of snowy mountain peaks, and the invigoration of pure mountain air, can imagine the joy with which I found myself in Switzerland on a sketching tour. It had not been easy for me to make this, my first visit to Europe. Circumstances, which the very slightly opened purses of my patrons had not enabled me to control, had deferred it for several years. And even now my stay was strictly limited, and I must return by a steamer which sailed for America early in the autumn. But I had already travelled a good deal on the Continent; had seen Italy; and now had six summer weeks to give to Switzerland. Six months would have suited me much better, but youth and enthusiasm can do a great deal of sketching and nature-revelling in six weeks.

I began what I called my Alpine holidays
in a little town not far from the upper end
of Lake Geneva, and at the close of my
second day of rambling and sketching I
was attacked by a very disagreeable and
annoying pain in my left leg. It did not
result, so far as I could ascertain, from a
sprain, a bruise, or a break, but seemed to
be occasioned by a sort of tantalising rheumatism; for while it entirely disappeared
when I remained at rest, its twinges began
as soon as I had taken half a dozen steps in
walking. The next day I consulted a doctor,
and he gave me a lotion. This, however,
was of no service, and for three or four days
he made use of other remedies, none of which
were of the slightest benefit to me.

But, although I was confined to the house
during this period, I did not lose my time.
From the windows of my room in the hotel
I had a series of the most enchanting views,
which I sketched from early morning until
twilight, with an earnest and almost ecstatic
zeal. On the other side of the lake rose, ten
thousand feet in the air, the great Dent du
Midi, with its seven peaks clear and sharp
against the sky, surrounded by its sister
mountains, most of them dark of base and
white of tip. To the east stretched the

beautiful valley of the Rhone, up which
the view extended to the pale-blue pyramid
of Mont Vélan. Curving northward around
the end of the lake was a range of lower
mountains, rocky or verdant; while at their
base, glistening in the sun, lay the blue lake
reflecting the white clouds in the sky, and
dotted here and there with little vessels,
their lateen-sails spread out like the wings
of a descending bird.

I sketched and painted the lake and
mountains, by the light of morning, in their
noontide splendours, and when all lay in
shadow except where the highest snowy
peaks were tipped with the rosy afterglow.
My ailment gave me no trouble at all so
long as I sat still and painted, and in the
wonderful opportunity afforded by nature
to my art I forgot all about it.

But in the course of a week I began to
get very impatient. There was a vast deal
more of Switzerland to be seen and sketched;
my time was growing short, and the pain
occasioned by walking had not abated in
the least. I felt that I must have other
views than those which were visible from my
window, and I had myself driven to various
points accessible to vehicles, from which I
made some very satisfactory sketches. But

this was not roaming in Alpine valleys and
climbing mountain peaks. It was only a
small part of what brought me to Switzerland, and my soul rebelled. Could any
worse fate befall a poor young artist, who
had struggled so hard to get over here, than
to be thus chained and trammelled in the
midst of the grandest opportunities his art
life had yet known?

My physician gave me but little comfort.
He assured me that if I used his remedies
and had patience, there would be no doubt
of my recovery; but that it would take
time. When I eagerly asked how much
time would be required, he replied that it
would probably be some weeks before I was
entirely well, for these disorders generally
wore off quite gradually.

"Some weeks!" I ejaculated when he
had gone. "And I have barely a month
left for Switzerland!"

This state of affairs not only depressed
me, but it disheartened me. I might have
gone by rail to other parts of Switzerland,
and made other sketches from hotels and
carriages, but this I did not care to do. If
I must still carry about with me my figura-
tive ball and chain, I did not wish to go
where new temptations would beckon and

call and scream to me from every side.
Better to remain where I was; where I
could more easily become used to my gall-
ing restraints. This was morbid reasoning,
but I had become morbid in body and mind.

One evening I went in the hotel omnibus
to the Kursaal of the little town where I
was staying. In this building, to which
visitors from the hotels and *pensions* of the
vicinity went in considerable numbers every
afternoon and evening, for the reason that
they had nothing else to do, the usual con-
cert was going on in the theatre. In a
small room adjoining, a company of gentlemen and ladies, the latter chiefly English or
Russian, were making bets on small metal
horses and jockeys which spun round on
circular tracks, and ran races which were
fairer to the betters than the majority of
those in which flesh-and-blood animals,
human and equine, take part. Opening
from this apartment was a large refresh-
ment-room, in which I took my seat. Here
I could smoke a cigar and listen to the
music, and perhaps forget for a time the
doleful world in which I lived. I had not
been long seated before I was joined by a
man whom I had met before, and in whom
I had taken some interest. He was a little

man with a big head, on which he occasionally wore a high-crowned black straw hat;
but whenever the sun did not make it absolutely necessary he carried this in his hand.
His clothes were black and of very thin
material, and he always had the appearance
of being too warm. In my occasional interviews with him I had discovered that he
was a reformer, and that his yearnings in
the direction of human improvement were
very general and inclusive.

This individual sat down at my little table
and ordered a glass of beer.

"You do not look happy," he said.
"Have you spoiled a picture?"

"No," I replied, "but a picture has been
spoiled for me." And, as he did not understand this reply, I explained to him how
the artistic paradise which I had mentally
painted for myself had been scraped from
the canvas by the knife of my malicious
ailment.

"I have been noticing," he said,—he spoke
very fair English, but it was not his native
tongue,—"that you have not walked. It is
a grand pity." And he stroked his beard
and looked at me steadfastly. "An artist
who is young is free," he said, after some
moments' reflection. "He is not obliged to

carry the load of a method which has grown upon him like the goitre of one of these people whom you meet here. He can despise methods and be himself. You have everything in art before you, and it is not right that you should be held to the ground like a serpent in your own country, with a forked stick. You have some friends, perhaps?"

I replied, a little surprised, that I had a great many friends in America.

"It is of no import where they are," he said. And then he again regarded me in silence. "Have you a good faith?" he presently asked.

"In what?" said I.

"In anything. Yourself, principally."

I replied that just now I had very little faith of that sort.

His face clouded; he frowned, and, pushing away his empty glass, he rose from the table. "You are a sceptic," he said, "and an infidel of the worst sort."

In my apathetic state this remark did not annoy me. "No man would be a sceptic," I said carelessly, "if other people did not persist in disagreeing with him."

But my companion paid no attention to me, and walked away before I had finished speaking. In a few minutes he came back, and, leaning over the table, he said in low but excited tones, "It is to yourself that you are an infidel. That is very wrong. It is degrading."

"I do not understand you at all," I said. "Won't you sit down and tell me what you mean?"

He seated himself, and wiped his forehead with his handkerchief. Then he fixed his eyes upon me, and said, "It is not to everybody I would speak as I now speak to you. You must believe something. Do you not believe in the outstretching power of the mind; of the soul?"

My ideas in this regard were somewhat chaotic. I did not know what was his exact meaning, but I thought it best to say that it was likely that some souls could outstretch.

"And do you not believe," he continued, "that when your friend sleeps, and your thoughts are fixed upon him, and your whole soul goes out to him in its most utter force and strength, that your mind becomes his mind?"

I shook my head. "That is going rather far," I said.

"It is not far," he exclaimed emphati-

cally. "It is but a little way. We shall
go much further than that when we know
more. And is it that you doubt that the
mind is in the brain? And where is pain?
Is it in the foot? In the arm? It is not
so. It is in the brain. If you cut off your
wounded foot, you have the pain all the
same; the brain remains. I will say this
to you. If it were I who had soul-friends,
it would not be that every day I should
shut the door on my art. Once it happened
that I suffered—not like you, much worse.
But I did not suffer every day. No, no, my
friend, not every day. But that was I; I
have faith. But I need speak no more to
you. You are infidel. You do not believe
in yourself."

And with this he suddenly pushed back
his chair, picked up his black straw hat
from the floor, and walked out of the room,
wiping his forehead as he went. I am not
given to sudden reciprocations of sentiment,
but what this man had said made a strong
impression upon me. Not that I had any
confidence in the value of his psychological
ideas, but his words suggested a train of
thought which kept me awake a long time
after I had gone to bed that night; and
gradually I began to consider the wonderful

B M B

advantage and help it would be to me if it were possible that a friend could bear my infirmity even for a day. It would inconvenience him but little. If he remained at rest he would feel no pain, and he might be very glad to be obliged to take a quiet holiday with his books or family. And what a joy would that holiday be to me among the Alps, and relieved of my fetters! The notion grew. One day one friend might take up my burden, and the next another. How little this would be for them; how much for me! If I should select thirty friends, they could, by each taking a day of pleasant rest, make me free to enjoy to the utmost the month which yet remained for Switzerland. My mind continued to dwell on this pleasing fancy, and I went to sleep while counting on my fingers the number of friends I had who would each be perfectly willing to bear for a day the infirmity which was so disastrous to me, but which would be of such trifling importance to them.

I woke very early in the morning, and my thoughts immediately recurred to the subject of my ailment and my friends. What a pity it was that such an advantageous arrangement should be merely whim and fancy! But if my companion of the

night before were here, he would tell me
that there was no impossibility, only a want
of faith—faith in the power of mind over
mind, of mind over body, and, primarily,
of faith in my own mind and will. I smiled
as I thought of what might happen if his
ideas were based on truth. There was my
friend Will Troy. How gladly would he
spend a day at home in his easy-chair,
smoking his pipe and forgetting, over a
novel, that there were such things as led-
gers, day-books, and columns of figures,
while I strode gaily over the mountain-
sides. If Troy had any option in the
matter, he would not hesitate for a moment;
and, knowing this, I would not hesitate for
a moment in making the little arrangement, ·
if it could be made. If belief in myself
could do it, it would be done ; and I began
to wonder if it were possible, in any case, for
a man to believe in himself to such an extent.

Suddenly I determined to try. "It is
early morning here," I said to myself, "and
in America it must be about the middle of
the night, and Will Troy is probably sound
asleep. Let me then determine, with all
the energy of my mental powers, that my
mind shall be his mind, and that he shall
understand thoroughly that he has some

sort of trouble in his left leg which will not inconvenience him at all if he allows it to rest, but which will hurt him very much if he attempts to walk about. Then I will make up my mind, quite decidedly, that for a day it shall be Will who will be subject to this pain, and not I."

For half an hour I lay flat on my back, my lips firmly pressed together, my hands clenched, and my eyes fixed upon the immutable peaks of the Dent du Midi, which were clearly visible through the window at the foot of my bed. My position seemed to be the natural one for a man bending all the energies of his mind on a determinate purpose. The great mountain stood up before me as an example of the steadfast and immovable. "Now," said I to myself, over and over again, "Will Troy, it is you who are subject to this trouble. You will know exactly what it is, because you will feel it through my mind. I am free from it; I will that, and it shall be so. My mind has power over your mind, because yours is asleep and passive, while mine is awake and very, very active. When I get out of bed I shall be as entirely free from pain and difficulty in walking as you would have been if I had not passed my condition over to you for one short day." And I repeated again and again—"For one day; only for one day."

The most difficult part of the process was the mental operation of believing all this. If I did not believe it, of course, it would come to nothing. Fixing my mind stead-fastly upon this subject, I believed with all my might. When I had believed for ten or fifteen minutes, I felt sure that my faith in the power of my mind was well grounded and fixed. A man who has truly believed for a quarter of an hour may be considered to have embraced a faith.

And now came the supreme moment, and when I arose should I be perfectly well and strong? The instant this question came in-to my mind I dismissed it. I would have no doubt whatever on the subject. I would *know* that I should be what I willed I should be. With my mind and my teeth firmly set, I got out of bed, I walked boldly to the window, I moved about the room, I dressed myself. I made no experiments; I would scorn to do so. Experiments imply doubt. I believed. I went down several flights of stairs to my breakfast. I walked the whole length of the long *salle-à-manger*, and sat down at the table without having felt a twinge of pain or the least discomfort.

"Monsieur is better this morning," said the head-waiter, with a kindly smile.

"Better," said I ; "I am well."

When I returned that evening after a day of intoxicating delight, during which I had climbed many a mountain path, had stood on bluffs and peaks, had gazed over lake and valley, and had breathed to the full the invigorating upper air, I stood upon the edge of the lake, just before reaching the hotel, and stretched forth my hands to the west.

"I thank you, Will Troy," I said, "from the bottom of my heart I thank you for this day ; and if I ever see my way to repay you, I will do it, my boy. You may be sure of that."

I now resolved to quit this place instantly. I had been here too long ; and before me was spread out in shadowy fascination the whole of Switzerland. I took a night-train for Berne, where I arrived early the next day. But before I descended from the railway carriage, where I had managed to slumber for part of the night, I had determinately willed an interchange of physical condition with another friend in America. During the previous day I had fully made up my mind that I

should be false to myself and to my fortunes if I gave up this grand opportunity
for study and artistic development, and I
would call upon my friends to give me
these precious holidays, of which, but a
little while ago, I believed myself for ever
deprived. I belonged to a club of artists,
most of whom were young and vigorous
fellows, any one of whom would be glad to
do me a service ; and although I desired on
special occasions to interchange with particular friends, I determined that during the
rest of my holiday I would, for the most
part, exchange physical conditions with
these young men, giving a day to each.

The next week was a perfect success. As
Martyn, Jeffries, Williams, Corbell, Field,
Booker, and Graham, I walked, climbed,
sketched, and, when nobody was near,
shouted with delight. I took Williams
for Sunday, because I knew he never
sketched on that day, although he was not
averse to the longest kind of rural ramble.
I shall not detail my route. The Bernese
Oberland, the region of Lake Lucerne, the
Engadine, and other earthly heavens opened
their doors to my joyous anticipations, provided always that this system of physical
exchange continued to work.

The Monday after Williams's Sunday I appropriated to a long tramp which should begin with a view of the sunrise from a mountain height, and which necessitated my starting in the morning before daylight. For such an excursion I needed all the strength and endurance of which I could possess myself, and I did not hesitate as to the exchange I should make for that long day's work. Chester Parkman was the man for me. Parkman was a fairly good artist, but the sphere in which he shone was that of the athlete. He was not very tall, but he was broad and well made, with a chest and muscles which to some of his friends appeared to be in an impertinent condition of perfect development. He was a handsome fellow, too, with his well-browned face, his fine white teeth, and his black hair and beard, which seemed to curl because the strength which they imbibed from him made it necessary to do something, and curling is all that hair can do. On some occasions it pleased me to think that when by the power of my will my physical incapacity was transferred for a time to a friend, I, in turn, found myself in his peculiar bodily condition, whatever it might be. And whether I was mistaken or not, and whether this phase of my borrowed condition was real or imaginary, it is certain that when I started out before dawn that Monday morning I strode away with vigorous Parkmanic legs, and inhaled the cool air into what seemed to be a deep Parkmanic chest. I took a guide that day, and when we returned, some time after nightfall, I could see that he was tired, and he admitted the fact; but as for me, I ate a good supper, and then walked a mile and a half to sketch a moonlight effect on a lake. I will here remark that, out of justice to Parkman, I rubbed myself down and polished myself off to the best of my knowledge and ability before I went to bed.

When, as usual, I awoke early the next morning, I lay for some time thinking. It had been my intention to spend that day in a boat on the lake, and I had decided to direct my will-power upon Tom Latham, a young collegian of my acquaintance. Tom was an enthusiastic oarsman, and could pull with such strength that if he were driving a horse he could almost haul the animal back into the vehicle, but if a stout boy were to be pushed off a horse-block Tom could not do it. Tom's unequally developed muscles were just what I wanted that day; but before I threw out my mind in his direction I let it dwell in pleasant recollection upon the glorious day I had had with Chester Parkman's corporeal attributes. Thinking of Chester, I began to think of some one else —one on whom my thoughts had rested with more pleasure and more pain than on any other person in the world. That this was a woman I need not say. She was young, she was an artist, and a very good friend of mine. For a long time I had yearned with all my heart to be able to say that she was more than this. But so far I could not say it. Since I had been in Europe I had told myself over and over that in coming away without telling Kate Balthis that I loved her I made the greatest mistake of·my life. I had intended to do this, but opportunity had not offered. I should have made opportunity.

The reason that the thought of Chester Parkman made me think of Kate was the fact that they occupied studios in the same building, and that he was a great admirer not only of her work, but of herself. If it had not been for the existence of Parkman, I should not have blamed myself quite so much for not proposing to Kate before I left America. But I consoled myself by reflecting that the man was so intent upon

the development of his lungs that his heart,
to put it anatomically, was obliged to take
a minor place in his consideration.

Thinking thus, a queer notion came into
my head. Suppose that Kate were to bear
my troubles for a day! What friend had I
who would be more willing to serve me than
she? And what friend from whom I would
be more delighted to receive a favour? But
the next instant the contemptibleness of
this idea flashed across my mind, and I
gritted my teeth as I thought what a despicable thing it would be to deprive that dear
girl of her strength and activity, even for a
day. It was true, as I honestly told myself, that it was the joy and charm of being
beholden to her, and not the benefit to myself, that made me think of this thing. But
it was despicable, all the same, and I utterly
scouted it. And so, forgetting as far as
possible that there was such a person in the
world as Kate, I threw out my mind, as I
originally intended, towards Tom Latham,
the oarsman.

I spent that day on the lake. If I had
been able to imagine that I could walk as
far as ·Chester Parkman, I failed to bring
myself to believe that I could row like
young Latham. I got on well enough, but

rowed no better than I had often done at
home, and I was soon sorry that I had
not brought a man with me to take the
oars, of which I had tired.

Among those I called upon in the next
few days was Professor Dynard, a man who
was not exactly a friend, but with whom I
was very well acquainted. He was a scientific man, a writer of books, and an enthusiastic lover of nature. He was middle-aged
and stooped a little, but his legs were long,
and he was an unwearied walker. Towards
the end of the very pleasant day which I
owed to my acquaintance with him, I could
not help smiling to find that I had thought
so much of the professor during my rambles
that I had unconsciously adopted the stoop
of his shoulder and his ungainly but regular
stride.

The half-starved man to whom food is
given eats too much ; the child, released
from long hours of school, runs wild, and is
apt to make himself objectionable ; and I,
rising from my condition of what I had considered hopeless inactivity to the fullest
vigour of body and limb, began to perceive
that I had walked too much and worked too
little. The pleasure of being able to ramble
and scramble wherever I pleased had made

me forget that I was in Switzerland not only for enjoyment, but for improvement. Of course I had to walk and climb to find points of view, but the pleasure of getting to such places was so great that it overshadowed my interest in sitting down and going to work after I had reached them. The man who sketches as he walks and climbs is an extraordinary artist, and I was not such an one.

It was while I was in the picturesque regions of the Engadine that these reflections forced themselves upon me, and I determined to live less for mere enjoyment and more for earnest work. But not for a minute did I think of giving up my precious system of corporeal exchange. I had had enough of sitting in my room and sketching from the window. If I had consented to allow myself to relapse into my former condition, I feared that I should not be able to regain that firm belief in the power of my mental propulsion which had so far enabled my friends to serve me so well, with such brief inconvenience to themselves. No. I would continue to transfer my physical incapacity, but I would use more conscientiously and earnestly the opportunities which I thus obtained.

Soon after I came to this determination, I established myself at a little hotel on a mountain-side, where I decided to stay for a week or more and do some good hard work ; I was surrounded by grand and beautiful scenery, and it was far better for my progress in art to stay here and do something substantial than to wander about in search of fresh delights. As an appropriate beginning to this industrious period, I made an exchange with my friend Bufford, one of the hardest-working painters I knew. His industry as well as his genius had brought him, when he had barely reached middle life, to a high position in art, and it pleased me to think that I might find myself influenced by some of his mental characteristics as well as those of a physical nature. At any rate, I tried hard to think so, and I am not sure that I did not paint better on the Bufford day than on any other. If it had not been that I had positively determined that I would not impose my ailment upon any one of my friends for more than one day, I would have taken Bufford for a week.

There were a good many people staying at the hotel, and among them was a very pretty English girl, with whom I soon became acquainted ; for she was an enthusi-

astic amateur artist, and was engaged in
painting the same view at which I had
chosen to work. Every morning she used
to go some distance up the mountain-side,
accompanied by her brother Dick, a tall,
gawky boy of about eighteen, who was considered to be a suitable and sufficient escort,
but who was in reality a very poor one, for
no sooner was his sister comfortably seated
at her work than he left her and rambled
away for hours. If it had not been for me
I think she would sometimes have been entirely too lonely and unprotected. Dick's
appetite would generally bring him back
in time to carry down her camp-chair and
colour-box when we returned to dinner;
and as she never complained of his defec-
tions, I suppose her mother knew nothing
about them. This lady was a very pleasant
person, a little too heavy in body and a little
too large in cap for my taste, but hearty and
genial, and very anxious to know something
about America, where her oldest son was
established on a Texas ranch. She and her
daughter and myself used to talk a good
deal together in the evenings, and this intimacy made me feel quite justified in talking
a good deal to the daughter in the mornings
as we were working together on the moun-

tain-side.   The first thing that made me
take an interest in this girl was the fact
that she considered me her superior, and
looked up to me. I could paint a great deal
better than she could, and could inform her
on a lot of points, and I was always glad to
render her such service.   She was a very
pretty girl, — the prettiest English girl I
ever saw,—with large, grey-blue eyes, which
had a trustfulness about them which I liked
very much.   She evidently had a very good
opinion of me as an artist, and paid as much
earnest and thoughtful attention to what I
said about her work as if she had really
been the scholar and I the master.   I tried
not to bore her by too much technical conversation, and endeavoured to make myself
as agreeable a companion as I could.   I
found that fellowship of some kind was
very necessary to a man so far away from
home, and so cut off from social influences.

Day after day we spent our mornings together, sketching and talking ; and as for
Dick, he was the most interesting brother I
ever knew. He had a great desire to discover something hitherto unknown in the
heights above our place of sketching. Finding that he could depend on me as a protector
for his sister, he gave us very little of his

company. Even when we were not together
I could not help thinking a great deal about
this charming girl. Our talks about her
country had made me remember with pride
the English blood that was in me, and re-
vived the desire I had often felt to live for a
time, at least, in rural England, that land of
loveliness to the Anglo-Saxon mind. And
London too! I had artist friends, Americans, who lived in London, and such were
their opportunities, such the art atmosphere
and society, that they expected to live there
always. If a fellow really wished to succeed
as an artist, some years' residence in England, with an occasional trip to the Continent, would be a great thing for him. And,
in such a case — well, it was a mere idle
thought. If I had been an engaged man,
I would not have allowed myself even such
idle thoughts. But I was not engaged; and
alas! I thought with a sigh, I might never
be. I thought of Parkman and of Kate,
and how they must constantly see each
other; and I remembered my stupid silence
when leaving America. How could I tell
what had happened since my departure? I
did not like to think of all this, and tried to
feel resigned. The world was very wide.
There was that English brother, over on the

Texas ranch; he might marry an American
girl; and here was his sister—well, this was
all the merest nonsense, and I would not
admit to myself that I attached the slightest
importance to these vague and fragmentary
notions which floated through my mind. But
the girl had most lovely, trustful eyes, and I
felt that a sympathy had grown up between
us which must not be rudely jarred.

We had finished our work at the old
sketching-place, and we proposed on the
morrow to go to a higher part of the mountain, and make some sketches of a more
extended nature than we had yet tried.
This excursion would require a good part
of the day, but we would take along a
luncheon for three, and no doubt nothing
would please Dick better than such a trip.
The mother agreed, if Dick could be made
to promise that he would take his sister by
the hand when he came to any steep places.
But, alas! when that youngster was called
upon to receive his injunctions, he declared
he could not accompany us. He had promised, he said, to go on a tramp with some
of the other men, which would take him all
day. And that, of course, put an end to
our expedition. I shall not soon forget the
air, charming to me, of evident sorrow and

disappointment with which Beatrice told
me this early in the evening. The next day
was the only one for which such a trip could
be planned, for, on the day following, two
older sisters were expected, and then everything would be different. I, too, was very
much grieved and disappointed, for I had
expected a day of rare pleasure ; but my regret was tempered by an intense satisfaction
at perceiving how sorry she was. The few
words she said on the subject touched me
very much. She was such a true, honest-
hearted girl that she could not conceal what
she felt ; and when we shook hands in bid-
ding each other good-night, it was with
more warmth than either of us had yet
shown at the recurrence of this little ceremony. When I went to my room I said to
myself : "If she had not been prevented
from going, I should never have known how
glad she would be to go." The thought
pleased me greatly, but I had no time to
dwell upon it, for in came Dick, who, with
his hands in his pockets and his legs very
wide apart, declared to me that he had found
his sister was so cut up by not being able
to make those sketches on the mountain the
next day, that he had determined to go
with us.

"It will be a beastly shame to disappoint her," he said ; "so you can get your traps together, and we will have an early break-fast and start off."

"Now," said I, when he had shut the door behind him, "I know how much she wanted to go, and she is going! Could any-thing be better than this?"

In making the physical transfers which were necessary at this period for my enjoy-ment of an outdoor excursion, I did not always bring my mental force to work upon an exchange of condition. Very often I was willing to send out my ailment to another, and to content myself with being for the day what I would be in my ordinary health. But in particular instances, such as those of Park-man and Bufford, I willed—and persuaded myself that I had succeeded—that certain desirable attributes of my benefactor for the day, which would be useless to him during his period of enforced restfulness, should be attracted to myself. Before I went to sleep I determined that on the following day I would exchange with my brother Philip, and would make it as absolute an exchange as my will could bring about. Phil was not an athlete, like Parkman, but he was a strong and vigorous fellow, with an immense

deal of go in him. He was thoroughly good-
natured, and I knew that he would be perfectly willing, if he could know all about it,
to take a day's rest, and give me a day with
Beatrice. And what a charming day that
was to be! We did not know exactly where
we were going, and we should have to ex-
plore. There would be steep places to climb,
and it would not be Dick who would help
his sister. We should have to rest, and we
would rest together. There would be a delightful lunch under the shade of some rock.
There would be long talks, and a charming
co-operation in the selection of points of
view and in work. Indeed, there was no
knowing what might not come out of a day
like that.

In the morning I made the transfer, and
soon afterwards I arose. Before I was ready
to go downstairs I was surprised by an attack of headache, a thing very unusual with
me. The pain increased so much that I was
obliged to go back to bed. I soon found
that I must give up the intended excursion,
and I remained in bed all day. In the
course of the afternoon, while I lay bemoan-
ing my present misery as well as the loss of
the great pleasure I had expected, a thought
suddenly came into my mind, which, in spite

of my miseries, made me burst out laughing. I remembered that my brother Phil, although enjoying, as a rule, the most vigorous good health, was subject to occasional attacks of sick headache, which usually laid him up for a day or two. Evidently I had struck him on one of his headache days. How relieved the old fellow must be to find his positive woe changed to a negative evil! It was very funny!

In the evening came Dick with a message from his mother and his sister Beatrice, who wanted to know how I felt by this time, and if I would have a cup of tea, or anything. "It's a beastly shame," said he, "that you got yourself knocked up in this way."

"Yes," said I, "but my misfortune is your good fortune, for, of course, you had your tramp with your friends."

"Oh, I should have had that any way," replied the good youth, "for I only intended to walk a mile or two up the mountain, just to satisfy the old lady, and then, without saying whether I was coming back or not, I intended to slip off and join the other fellows. Wouldn't that have been a jolly plan? Beatrice would have had her day, and I should have had mine. But *you* must go and upset her part of it."

When Dick had gone I reflected. What a day this would have been ! Alone so long with Beatrice among those grand old mountains ! As I continued to think of this I began to tremble, and the more I thought the more I trembled ; and the reason I trembled was the conviction that if I had spent that day with her, I certainly should have proposed to her.

"Phil," I said, "I thank you. I thank you more for your headache than for anything else any other fellow could give me."

A sick headache, aided by conscience, can work a great change in a man. My soul condemned me for having come so near being a very false lover, and my mind congratulated me upon having the miss made for me, for I never should have been strong enough to make it for myself.

The next day the sisters arrived, and I saw but little of Beatrice, for which, although quite sorry, I was also very glad ; and after a day on the mountain which I owed to Horace Bartlett, the last man in our club on whom I felt I could draw, I returned to the hotel, and wrote a long letter to Kate. I had informed my friends in America of the ailment which had so frustrated all my plans of work and enjoyment, but I had

never written anything in regard to my
novel scheme of relief. This was something which could be better explained by
word of mouth when I returned. And, besides, I did not wish to say anything about
it until the month of proposed physical
transfers had expired. I wrote to Kate,
however, that I was now able to walk and
climb as much as I pleased, and in my
repentant exuberance I hinted at a great
many points which, although I knew she
could not understand them, would excite
her curiosity and interest in the remarkable story I would tell her when I returned.
I tried to intimate, in the most guarded
way, much that I intended to say to her
when I saw her concerning my series of
deliverances ; and my satisfaction at having
escaped a great temptation gave a kindly
earnestness to my manner of expressing myself, which otherwise it might not have had.

There were now six days of my Swiss
holiday left; and during these I threw
myself upon the involuntary kindness of
Mr. Henry Brinton, editor of a periodical
entitled "Our Mother Earth," and upon
that of his five assistants in the publishing
and editorial departments. Brinton was a
good fellow, devoted to scientific agricul-

ture and the growing of small fruits ; a man of a most practical mind. I knew him and his associates very well, and had no hesitation in calling upon them.

At the end of the month, as I had previously resolved, I brought my course of physical transfers to a close; and it was with no little anxiety that I arose one morning from my bed with my mind determined to bear in my own proper person all the ills of which I was possessed.

I walked across the room. It may appear strange, but I must admit that it was with a feeling of satisfaction that I felt a twinge. It was but a little twinge, but yet I felt it, and this was something that had not happened to me for a month.

"It was not fancy, then," I said to myself, "that gave me this precious relief, this month of rare delight and profit ; it was the operation of the outstretching power of the mind. I owe you much happiness, you little man with the big head whom I met in the Kursaal, and if you were here I would make you admit that I can truly believe in myself."

The next day I was better, with only an occasional touch of the old disorder : and in a few days I was free from it altogether, and could walk as well as ever I could in my life.

I returned to America strong and agile, and with a portfolio full of suggestive sketches. One of these was the back hair and part of the side face of a girl who was engaged in sketching in a mountainous region. But this I tore up on the voyage.

WEST.

I WILL now relate the events which took place in America, among the people in whom I was most interested, while I, a few thousand miles to the east, was enjoying my month of excursion and art work in the mountains of Switzerland.

On my return to my old associates I had intended to state to all of them, in turn, that I owed my delightful holiday to the fact that I had been able to transfer to them the physical disability which had prevented me from making use of the opportunities offered me by the Alps and the vales of Helvetia. But by conversation with one and another I gradually became acquainted with certain interesting facts which determined me to be very cautious in making disclosures regarding the outreaching power of my will.

No one of my friends was so much affected by my departure for Europe as that dear girl Kate Balthis, although I had no idea

at the time that this was so. It was not
that she was opposed to my going ; on the
contrary, it was she who had most encouraged me to persevere in my intention to
visit Europe, and to conquer or disregard
the many obstacles to the plan which rose
up before me. She had taken a great interest in my artistic career, and much more
personal interest in me than I had dared to
suppose. She had imagined, and I feel that
she had a perfect right to do so, that I felt
an equal interest in her ; and when I went
away without a word more than any friend
might say to another, the girl was hurt. It
was not a deep wound ; it was more in the
nature of a rebuff. She felt a slight sense
of humiliation, and wondered if she had
infused more warmth into her intercourse
with me than was warranted by the actual
quality of our friendship. But she cherished
no resentment, and merely put away an
almost finished interior, in which I had
painted a fair but very distant landscape
seen through a partly opened window, and
set herself to work on a fresh canvas.

Chester Parkman, the artist-athlete, whom
I have mentioned, was always fond of Kate's
society ; but after my departure he came a
great deal more frequently to her studio

than before ; and he took it into his head
that he would like to have his portrait
painted by her. I had never supposed
that Parkman's mind was capable of such
serviceable subtlety as this, and I take
the opportunity here to give him credit for
it. Kate's forte was clearly portraiture,
although she did not confine herself at
that time to this class of work ; and she
was well pleased to have such an admirable subject as Chester Parkman, who,
if he had not been an artist himself, might
have made a very comfortable livelihood by
acting as a model for other artists. This
portrait-painting business, of which I should
have totally disapproved had I known of it,
brought them together for an hour every
day ; and, although Kate had two or three
pupils, they worked in an adjoining room,
separated by drapery from her own studio ;
and this gave Parkman every opportunity
of making himself as agreeable as he could
be. His method of accomplishing this, I
have reason to believe, was by looking as
well as he could rather than by conversa-
tional efforts. But he made Kate agreeable
to him in a way of which at the time she
knew nothing. He so arranged his position
that a Venetian mirror in a corner gave

him an admirable view of Kate's face as she sat at her easel. Thus, as she studied his features, his eyes dwelt more and more fondly upon hers, though she noticed it not. This sort of thing went on till Parkman found himself in a very bad way. The image of Kate rose up before him when he was not in her studio, and it had such an influence upon him that, if I may so put it, he gradually sunk his lungs, and let his heart rise to the surface. He imagined, though with what reason I am not prepared to say, that he could perceive in Kate's countenance indications of much admiration of her subject, and he flattered himself this was not confined to her consideration of him as a model. In fact, he found that he was very much in love with the girl. If he had been a wise man, he would have postponed proposing to her until his portrait was finished, for if she refused him he would lose both picture and painter. But he was not a wise man, and one day he made up his mind that as soon as she had finished the corner of his mouth, at which she was then at work, he would abandon his pose, and tell her how things stood with him. But a visitor came in, and prevented this plan from being carried out. This interruption, however, was merely a postponement. Parkman determined that on the next day he would settle the matter with Kate the moment he arrived at the studio, or as soon, at least, as he was alone with her.

If he had known the state of Kate's mind at this time, he would have been very much encouraged. I do not mean to say that any tenderness of sentiment towards him was growing up within her, but she had begun to admire very much this fine, handsome fellow. She took more pleasure in working at his portrait than in any other she had yet done. A man, she had come to think, to be true to art and to his manhood, should look like this one.

Thus it was that although Kate Balthis had not yet thought of her model with feelings that had become fond, it could not be denied that her affections, having lately been obliged to admit that they had no right to consider themselves occupied, were not in a condition to repel a new-comer. And Parkman was a man who, when he had made up his mind to offer his valued self, would do it with a vigour and earnestness that could not easily be withstood.

It was a long time before Chester Parkman went to sleep that night, so engaged was he in thinking upon what he was going to do on the morrow. But, shortly after he arose the next morning, he was attacked by a very queer feeling in his left leg, which made it decidedly unpleasant for him when he attempted to walk. Indisposition of any kind was exceedingly unusual with the young athlete, but he knew that under the circumstances the first thing necessary for his accurately developed muscles was absolute rest, and this he gave them. He sent a note to Kate, telling her what had happened to him, and expressing his great regret at not being able to keep his appointment for the day. He would see her, however, at the very earliest possible moment that this most unanticipated disorder would allow him. He sent for a trainer, and had himself rubbed and lotioned, and then betook himself to a pipe, a novel, and a big easy-chair, having first quieted his much-perturbed soul by assuring it that if he did not get over this thing in a few days, he would write to Kate, and tell her in the letter all he had intended to say.

The next day, much to his surprise, he arose perfectly well. He walked, he strode, he sprang into the air ; there was absolutely nothing the matter with him. He rejoiced beyond his power of expression, and determined to visit Kate's studio even earlier than the usual hour; but before he was ready to start he received a note from her, which stated that she had been obliged to stay at home that day on account of a sudden attack of something like rheumatism, and therefore, even if he thought himself well enough, he need not make the exertion necessary to go all the way up to her studio. This note was very prettily expressed, and on the first reading of it Parkman could see nothing in it but a kind desire on the part of the writer that he should know there would be no occasion for him to do himself a possible injury by mounting to her lofty studio before he was entirely recovered. Of course she could not know, he thought, that he would be able to come that day, but it was very good of her to consider the possible contingency.

But, after sitting down and reflecting on the matter for ten or fifteen minutes, Parkman took a different view of the note. He now perceived that the girl was making fun of him. What imaginable reason was there for believing that she, a perfectly healthy person, should be suddenly afflicted by a rheumatism which apparently was as much

like that of which he had told her the day
before as one pain could be like another.
Yes, she was making game of the muscles
and sinews on which he prided himself.
She did not believe the excuse he had given,
and trumped up this ridiculous ailment to
pay him back in his own coin. Chester
Parkman was not easily angered, but he
allowed this mote to touch him on a tender
point. It seemed to intimate that he would
asperse his own physical organisation in
order to get an excuse for not keeping an
appointment. To accuse him of such dis-
loyalty was unpardonable. He was very
indignant, and said to himself that he
would give Miss Balthis some time to come
to her senses ; and that if she were that
kind of a girl, it would be very well for him
to reflect. He wrote a coldly expressed
note to Kate, in which he said that, as far
as he was concerned, he would not inconvenience her by giving her even the slightest reason for coming to her studio during
the continuance of her most inexplicable
malady.

Mr. Chester Parkman's mind might have
been much more legitimately disturbed had
he known that during the night before Kate
had been lying awake, and had been think-

ing of me. She had heard that day from a
friend, to whom I had written, of the great
misfortune which had happened to me in
Switzerland ; and she had been thinking,
dear girl, that if it were possible how gladly
would she bear my trouble for a time, and
give me a chance to enjoy that lovely land
which I had tried so hard to reach. And if
he had been told that at that very time, as
I lay awake in the early morning, the idea
had come into my head, although most instantly dismissed, that I should like to be
beholden to Kate for a day of Alpine pleasure, he would reasonably have wondered
what that had to do with it.

After I had become acquainted with these
facts, I asked young Tom Latham, the oarsman, to whom I supposed I had transferred
my physical condition on the day after I
walked with Parkmanic legs to see the sun
rise, if he had been at all troubled with
rheumatism during the past few months.
He replied with some asperity that he had
been as right as a trivet straight along ; and
why in the world did I imagine he was subject to rheumatism !

Of course Kate was annoyed when she received Parkman's note. She saw that he
had taken offence at something, although

she had no idea what it was. But she did not allow this to trouble her long, and said to herself that if Mr. Parkman was angry with her she was very sorry, but she would be content to postpone work on the portrait until he should recover his good humour.

When she had retired that night she had determined that, if she should not be well enough to go to her studio in a few days, she would send for some of her working materials and try to paint in her room. But the next morning she arose perfectly well.

If, however, she had known what was going to happen, she would have preferred spending another day in her pleasant chamber with her books and sewing. For, about eleven o'clock in the morning, there walked into her studio Professor Dynard, a gentleman who for some time had taken a great deal of interest in her and her work.

She had usually been very well pleased to talk to him, for he was a man of wide information and good judgment. But this morning there seemed to be something about him which was not altogether pleasant. In the first place, he stood before the unfinished portrait of Chester Parkman, regarding it with evident displeasure. For some minutes he said nothing, but hemmed and grunted.

Presently he turned and remarked, "I don't like it."

"What is the matter with it?" asked Kate from the easel at which she was at work. "Have I not caught the likeness?"

"Oh, that is good enough as far as it goes," said the Professor. "Very good indeed! too good! You are going to make an admirable picture. But I wish you had another subject."

"Why, I thought myself extraordinarily fortunate in getting so good a one!" exclaimed Kate. "Is he not an admirable model?"

"Of course he is," said the Professor, "but I don't like to see you painting a young fellow like Parkman. Now, don't be angry," he continued, taking a seat near her and looking around to see if the curtain of the pupils' room was properly drawn. "I take a great interest in your welfare, Miss Balthis, and my primary object in coming here this morning is to tell you so; and, therefore, you must not be surprised that I was somewhat annoyed when I found that you were painting young Parkman's portrait. I don't like you to be painting the portraits of young men, Miss Balthis, and I will tell you why."

And then he drew his chair a little nearer to her, and offered himself in marriage.

It must be rather awkward for a young lady artist to be proposed to at eleven o'clock in the morning, when she is sitting at her easel, one hand holding her palette and maul-stick, and the other her brush, and with three girl pupils on the other side of some moderately heavy drapery, probably listening with all their six ears. But in Kate's case the peculiarity of the situation was emphasised by the fact that this was the first time that any one had ever proposed to her. She had expected me to do something of the kind; and two days before, although she did not know it, she had just missed a declaration from Parkman; but now it was really happening, and a man was asking her to marry him. And this man was Professor Dynard! Had Kate been in the habit of regarding him with the thousand eyes of a fly, never, with a single one of those eyes, would she have looked upon him as a lover. But she turned towards him, and sat up very straight, and listened to all he had to say.

The Professor told a very fair story. He had long admired Miss Balthis, and had ended by loving her. He knew very well that he was no longer a young man, but he thought that if she would carefully consider the matter, she would agree with him that he was likely to make her a much better husband than the usual young man could be expected to make. In the first place, the object of his life, as far as fortune was concerned, had been accomplished, and he was ready to devote the rest of his days to her, her fortune, and her happiness. He would not ask her to give up her art, but, on the contrary, would afford her every facility for work and study under the most favourable circumstances. He would take her to Europe, to the isles of the sea,—wherever she might like to go. She could live in the artistic heart of the world, or in any land where she might be happy. He was a man both able and free to devote himself to her. He had money enough, and he was not bound by circumstances to special work or particular place. Through him the world would be open to her, and his greatest happiness should be to see her enjoy her opportunities. "More than that," he continued, "I want you to remember that, although I am no longer in my first youth, I am very strong, and enjoy excellent health. This is something you should consider very carefully in making an

alliance for life ; for it would be most unfortunate for you if you should marry a man
who, early in life, should become incapaci-
tated from pursuing his career, and you
should find yourself obliged to provide, not
only for yourself, but for him."

This, Kate knew very well, was intended
as a reference to me. Professor Dynard had
reason to believe I was much attached to
Kate, and he had heard exaggerated accounts of my being laid up with rheumatism
in Switzerland. It was very good in him to
warn her against a man who might become
a chronic invalid on her hands ; but Kate
said nothing to him, and let him go on.

"And even these devotees of muscu-
larity," said the Professor, "these amateur
athletes, are liable to be stricken down at
any moment by some unforeseen disease.
I do not wish to elevate the body above the
mind, Miss Balthis, but these things should
be carefully considered. You should marry
a man who is not only in vigorous health,
but is likely to continue so. And now, my
dear Miss Balthis, I do not wish you to
utter one word in answer to what I have
been saying to you. I want you to consider, carefully and earnestly, the proposition I have made. Do not speak now, I

beg of you, for I know I could not expect at
this moment a favourable answer. I want
you to give your calm judgment an opportunity to come to my aid. On the day
after to-morrow I will come to receive your
answer. Good-bye."

During that afternoon and the next day
Kate thought of little but of the offer of
marriage which had been made to her.
Sometimes she regretted that she had not
been bold enough to interrupt him with a
refusal, and so end the matter. And then,
again, she fell to thinking upon the subject
of love, thinking and thinking. Naturally
her first thoughts fell upon me. But I had
not spoken, nor had I written. This could
not be accidental. It had a meaning which
she ought not to allow herself to overlook.
She found, too, while thus turning over the
contents of her mind, that she had thought
a little, a very little she assured herself,
about Chester Parkman. She admitted
that there was something insensibly attrac-
tive about him, and he had been extremely
attentive and kind to her. But even if her
thoughts had been inclined to dwell upon
him, it would have been ridiculous to allow
them to do so now, for in some way she had
offended him, and might never see him

again. He must be of a very irritable disposition.

And then there came up before her visions
of Europe and of the isles of the sea ; of a
life amid the art wonders of the world,—a
life with every wish gratified, every desire made possible. Professor Dynard had
worked much better than she had supposed
at the time he was working. He had not
offered her the kind of love she had expected, should love ever be offered, but he
had placed before her, immediately and
without reserve, everything to which she
had expected to attain by the labours of a
life. All this was very dangerous thinking
for Kate ; the fortifications of her heart
were being approached at a very vulnerable
point. When she started independently in
life, she did not set out with the determination to fall in love, or to have love made to
her, or to be married, or anything of the
kind. Her purpose was to live an art life ;
and to do that as she wished to do it, she
would have to work very hard and wait
very long. But now, all she had to do was
to give a little nod, and the hope of the future
would be the fact of the present. Even her
own self would be exalted. "What a different woman should I be," she thought,

"in Italy or in Egypt." This was a terribly perilous time for Kate. The temptation came directly into the line of her hopes and aspirations. It tinged her mind with a delicately spreading rosiness.

The next morning when she went to her studio she found there a note from Professor Dynard, stating that he could not keep his appointment with her that day on account of a sudden attack of something like rheumatism, which made it impossible to leave his room. This indisposition was not a matter of much importance, he wrote, and would probably disappear in a few days, when he would hasten to call upon her. He begged that in the meantime she would continue the consideration of the subject on which he had spoken to her; and hoped very earnestly that she would arrive at a conclusion which should be favourable to him, and which, in that case, he most sincerely believed would also be favourable to herself.

When she read this, Kate leaned back in her chair and laughed. "After all he said the other day about the danger of my getting a husband who would have to be taken care of, this is certainly very funny!" She forgot the rosy hues which had been insensibly tinting her dreams of the future on the day before, and only thought of a middle-aged gentleman, with a little bald place on the top of his head, who was subject to rheumatism, and probably very cross when he was obliged to stay in the house. "It is a shame," she said to herself, "to allow the poor old gentleman to worry his mind about me any longer. It will be no more than a deception to let him lie at home and imagine that as soon as he is well he can come up here and get a favourable answer from me. I'll write him a note immediately and settle the matter." And this she did, and thereby escaped the greatest danger to herself to which she had ever been exposed.

Nearly all Kate's art friends had been very much interested in her portrait of Chester Parkman, which, in its nearly completed state, was the best piece of work she had done. Among these friends was Bufford, whose pupil Kate had been, and to whom she had long looked up, not only as to a master, but as to a dear and kind friend. Mrs. Bufford, too, was extremely fond of Kate, and was ever ready to give her counsel and advice, but not in regard to art, which subject she resigned entirely to her husband. It was under Mrs. Bufford's guidance that Kate, when she first came to

the city from her home in the interior of
the State, selected her boarding-house, her
studio, and her church. More than half of
her Sundays were spent with these good
friends, and they had always considered it
their duty to watch over her as if her
parents had appointed them her guardians.
Bufford was greatly disappointed when he
found that the work on Parkman's portrait
had been abruptly broken off. He had
wished Kate to finish it in time for an approaching exhibition, where he knew it
would attract great attention, both from
the fact that the subject was so well known
in art circles and in society, and because it
was going to be, he believed, a most admirable piece of work. Kate had explained to
him, as far as she knew, how matters stood.
Mr. Parkman had suddenly become offended
with her, why she knew not. He was perfectly well and able to come, she said, for
some of her friends had seen him going
about as usual ; but he did not come to her,
and she certainly did not intend to ask him
to do so. Bufford shook his head a good
deal at this, and when he went home and
told his wife about it, he expressed his
opinion that Kate was not to blame in the
matter.

"That young Parkman," he said, "is extremely touchy, and he has an entirely too good opinion of himself; and by indulging in some of his cranky notions he is seriously . interfering with Kate's career, for she has nothing on hand except his portrait which I would care to have her exhibit."

"Now don't you be too sure," said Mrs. Bufford, "about Kate not being to blame. Young girls, without the slightest intention, sometimes do and say things which are very irritating, and Kate is just as high-spirited as Parkman is touchy. I have no doubt that the whole quarrel is about some ridiculous trifle, and could be smoothed over with a few words, if we could only get the few words said. I was delighted when I heard she was painting Chester's portrait, for I hoped the work would result in something much more desirable even than a good picture."

"I know you always wanted her to marry him," said Bufford.

"Yes, and I still want her to do so. And a little piece of nonsense like this should not be allowed to break off the best match I have ever known."

"Since our own," suggested her husband.

"That is understood," she replied. "And

now, do you know what I think is our duty in the premises? We should make it our business to heal this quarrel, and bring these young people together again. I am extremely anxious that no time should be lost in doing this, for it will not be long before young Clinton will be coming home. He was to stay away only three months altogether."

"And you are afraid he will interfere with your plans?" said Bufford.

"Indeed I am," answered his wife. "For a long time Kate and he have been very intimate,—entirely too much so,—and I was very glad when he went away, and gave poor Chester a chance. Of course there is nothing settled between them so far, because if there had been Clinton would never have allowed that portrait to be thought of."

"Jealous wretch!" remarked Bufford.

"You need not joke about it," said his wife. "It would be a most deplorable thing for Kate to marry Clinton. He has, so far, made no name for himself in art, and no one can say that he ever will. He is poor, and has nothing on earth but what he makes, and it is not probable that he will ever make anything. And, worse than all that, he has become a chronic invalid. I have heard about his condition in Switzerland."

"And having originally very little," said her husband, "and having lost the only valuable thing he possessed, you would take away from him even what he expected to have."

"He has no right to expect it," said Mrs. Bufford, "and it would be a wicked and cruel thing for him to endeavour to take Kate away from a man like Chester Parkman. Chester is rich, he is handsome, he is in perfect health, and to a girl with an artistic mind like Kate he should be a constant joy to look upon."

"But," said Bufford, "why don't you leave Kate to find out these superiorities for herself?"

"It would never do at all. Don't you see how she has let the right man go on account of some trifling misunderstanding? And Clinton will come home, and find that he has the field all to himself. Now I'll tell you what I want you to do. You must go to Kate to-morrow, find out what this trouble is about, and represent to her that she ought not to allow a little misunderstanding to interfere with her career in art."

"Why don't you go yourself?" said Bufford.

"That is out of the question. I could not
put the matter on an art basis, and anything
else would rouse Kate's suspicions. And,
besides, I want you afterwards to go to
Parkman, and talk to him ; and, of course,
I could not do that."

"Very well," said Bufford, "I am going
to see them both to-morrow, and will endeavour to make things straight between
them ; but I don't wish to be considered as
having anything to do with the matrimonial
part of the affair. What I want is to have
Kate finish that picture in time for the exhibition."

"You attend to that," said his wife,
"and the matrimonial part will take care
of itself."

But Bufford did not see either Kate or
Parkman the next day, being prevented
from leaving his room by a sudden attack
of something like rheumatism. He was a
man of strong good sense and persuasive
speech, and I think he would have had no
difficulty in bringing Parkman and Kate together again ; and if this had happened, I
am very certain that Parkman would have
lost no time in declaring his passion. What

would have resulted from this, of course, I cannot say ; but it must be remembered that Kate at that time supposed that she had made a great mistake in regard to my sentiments towards her. In fact, if Bufford had seen the two young people that day, I am afraid, I am very much afraid, that everything would have gone wrong.

The next day Bufford did see Kate, and easily obtained her permission to call on Parkman, and endeavour to find out what it was that had given him umbrage ; but as the young athlete had started that very morning for a trip to the West, Bufford was obliged to admit to himself, very reluctantly, that it was probably useless to consider any further the question of Kate's finishing his portrait in time for the exhibition.

When I returned to America, and at the very earliest possible moment presented myself before Kate, I had not been ten seconds in her company before I perceived that I was an accepted lover. How I perceived this I will not say, for every one who has been accepted can imagine it for himself ; but I will say that, although raised to the wildest pitch of joy by the discovery, I was very much surprised at it.

I had never told the girl I loved her. I had
never asked her to love me. But here it
was, all settled, and Kate was my own
dear love. Of course, feeling as I did towards her, it was easy for me to avoid any
backwardness of demeanour, which might
indicate to her that I was surprised, and I
know that not for a moment did she suspect it. Before the end of our interview,
however, I found out how I had been accepted without knowing it. It had been
on account of the letter I had written Kate
from Switzerland. In this very carefully
constructed epistle I had hinted at a great
many things which I had been careful not
to explain, not wishing to put upon paper
the story of my series of wonderful deliverances, which I intended with my own mouth
to tell to Kate. It was a subtly quiet letter,
with a substratum of hilariousness, of enthusiasm, surging beneath it, which sometimes showed through the thin places in
the surface. Of course, writing to Kate,
my mind was full of her, as well as of my
deliverances, and in my hypersubtlety I so
expressed my feelings in regard to the
latter of these subjects that it might easily
have been supposed to pertain to the first.
In fact, when I afterwards read this letter

I did not wonder at all that the dear girl thought it was a declaration of love. That she made the mistake I shall never cease to rejoice ; for, after leaving Switzerland, I should not have been able, involuntarily and unconsciously, to ward off until my return the attacks of possible lovers.

From day to day I met nearly all the persons who, without having the slightest idea that they were doing anything of the kind, had been of such wonderful service to me while I was abroad ; and I never failed to make particular inquiries in regard to their health the past summer. Most of them replied that they had been very well as a general thing, although now and then they might have been under the weather for a day or two. Few of my friends were people who were given to remembering ailments past and gone, and if I had needed any specific information from them in regard to any particular day on which they had been confined to the house by this or that slight disorder, I should not have obtained it.

But when I called upon Henry Brinton, the editor of "Our Mother Earth," I received some very definite and interesting information.

"Everything has gone on pretty much as usual since you left," he said, "except that about a month ago we had a visitation of a curious sort of epidemic rheumatism, which actually ran through the office. It attacked me first, but as I understand such things and know very well that outward applications are of no possible use, I took the proper medicine, and in one day, sir, I was entirely cured. The next day, however, Barclay, our book-keeper, was down with it, or, rather, he was obliged to stay at home on account of it. I immediately sent him my bottle of medicine, and the next day he came down to the office perfectly well. After him Brown, Simmons, Cummings, and White, one after another, were all attacked in the same way, but each was cured by my medicine in a day. The malady, however, seemed gradually to lose its force, and Cummings and White were only slightly inconvenienced, and were able to come to the office."

All this was very plain to me. Brinton's medicine was indeed the proper remedy for my ailment, and had gradually cured it, so that when I resumed it after my month's exemption, there was very little left of it, and this soon died out of itself.

If I could only have known this, I would
have sent it over to Brinton in the first
instance.

In the course of time I related to Kate
the strange series of incidents which had
finally brought us together. I am sorry to
say she did not place entire belief in the outreaching powers of my mind. She thought
that the relief from my disability was due
very much to imagination.

"How," I said, "do you account for
those remarkable involuntary holidays of
Parkman, yourself, and the others, which
were so opportune for me?"

"Things did happen very well for you,"
she said, "although I suppose a great many
other people have had a series of lucky events
come into their lives. But even if this were
all true, I do not think it turned out exactly
as it should have done in a moral point of
view. Of course I am delighted, you poor
boy, that you should have had that charming
month in Switzerland, after all the trouble
you had gone through; but wasn't it a little
selfish to pass off your disability upon your
friends without asking them anything about
it?"

"Well," said I, "it may be that if this
affair were viewed from a purely moral

standpoint, there was a certain degree of
selfishness about it, and it ought to have
turned out all wrong for me. But we live
in a real world, my dear, and it turned out
all right."

A TALE OF NEGATIVE
GRAVITY.

A TALE OF NEGATIVE GRAVITY.

MY wife and I were staying at a small town in northern Italy; and on a certain pleasant afternoon in spring we had taken a walk of six or seven miles to see the sun set behind some low mountains to the west of the town. Most of our walk had been along a hard, smooth highway, and then we turned into a series of narrower roads, sometimes bordered by walls, and sometimes by light fences of reed, or cane. Nearing the mountain, to a low spur of which we intended to ascend, we easily scaled a wall about four feet high, and found ourselves upon pasture land, which led, sometimes by gradual ascents, and sometimes by bits of rough climbing, to the spot we wished to reach. We were afraid we were a little late, and therefore hurried on, running up the grassy hills, and bounding briskly over the rough and rocky places. I carried a knapsack strapped firmly to my shoulders, and under my

wife's arm was a large, soft basket of a
kind much used by tourists. Her arm was
passed through the handles, and around the
bottom of the basket, which she pressed
closely to her side. This was the way she
always carried it. The basket contained
two bottles of wine, one sweet for my wife,
and another a little acid for myself. Sweet
wines give me a headache.

When we reached the grassy bluff, well
known thereabouts to lovers of sunset views,
I stepped immediately to the edge to gaze
upon the scene, but my wife sat down to
take a sip of wine, for she was very thirsty ;
and then, leaving her basket, she came to
my side. The scene was indeed one of
great beauty. Beneath us stretched a wide
valley of many shades of green, with a
little river running through it, and red-tiled
houses here and there. Beyond rose a
range of mountains, pink, pale-green, and
purple where their tips caught the reflection of the setting sun, and of a rich grey-
green in shadows. Beyond all was the blue
Italian sky, illumined by an especially fine
sunset.

My wife and I are Americans, and at the
time of this story were middle-aged people
and very fond of seeing in each other's

company whatever there was of interest or beauty around us. We had a son about twenty-two years old, of whom we were also very fond, but he was not with us, being at that time a student in Germany. Although we had good health, we were not very robust people, and, under ordinary circumstances, not much given to long country tramps. I was of medium size, without much muscular development, while my wife was quite stout, and growing stouter.

The reader may, perhaps, be somewhat surprised that a middle-aged couple, not very strong, or very good walkers, the lady loaded with a basket containing two bottles of wine and a metal drinking-cup, and the gentleman carrying a heavy knapsack, filled with all sorts of odds and ends, strapped to his shoulders, should set off on a seven-mile walk, jump over a wall, run up a hillside, and yet feel in very good trim to enjoy a sunset view. This peculiar state of things I will proceed to explain.

I had been a professional man, but some years before had retired upon a very comfortable income. I had always been very fond of scientific pursuits, and now made these the occupation and pleasure of much of my leisure time. Our home was in a

small town; and in a corner of my grounds
I built a laboratory, where I carried on my
work and my experiments. I had long been
anxious to discover the means, not only of
producing, but of retaining and controlling,
a natural force, really the same as centrifugal force, but which I called negative
gravity. This name I adopted because it
indicated better than any other the action
of the force in question, as I produced it.
Positive gravity attracts everything toward
the centre of the earth. Negative gravity,
therefore, would be that power which repels
everything from the centre of the earth, just
as the negative pole of a magnet repels the
needle, while the positive pole attracts it.
My object was, in fact, to store centrifugal
force, and to render it constant, controllable,
and available for use. The advantages of
such a discovery could scarcely be described.
In a word, it would lighten the burdens of
the world.

I will not touch upon the labours and dis-
appointments of several years. It is enough
to say that at last I discovered a method of
producing, storing, and controlling negative
gravity.

The mechanism of my invention was rather
complicated, but the method of operating it

was very simple. A strong metallic case, about eight inches long, and half as wide, contained the machinery for producing the force; and this was put into action by means of the pressure of a screw worked from the outside. As soon as this pressure was produced, negative gravity began to be evolved and stored, and the greater the pressure the greater the force. As the screw was moved outward, and the pressure diminished, the force decreased, and when the screw was withdrawn to its fullest extent, the action of negative gravity entirely ceased. Thus this force could be produced or dissipated at will to such degrees as might be desired, and its action, so long as the requisite pressure was maintained, was constant.

When this little apparatus worked to my satisfaction I called my wife into my laboratory and explained to her my invention and its value. She had known that I had been at work with an important object, but I had never told her what it was. I had said that if I succeeded I would tell her all, but if I failed she need not be troubled with the matter at all. Being a very sensible woman, this satisfied her perfectly. Now I explained everything to her, the construction of the machine, and the wonderful uses to which

this invention could be applied. I told her
that it could diminish, or entirely dissipate,
the weight of objects of any kind. A heavily
loaded wagon, with two of these instruments
fastened to its sides, and each screwed to a
proper force, would be so lifted and supported that it would press upon the ground
as lightly as an empty cart, and a small
horse could draw it with ease. A bale of
cotton, with one of these machines attached,
could be handled and carried by a boy. A
car, with a number of these machines, could
be made to rise in the air like a balloon.
Everything, in fact, that was heavy could
be made light ; and as a great part of labour,
all over the world, is caused by the attraction of gravitation, so this repellent force,
wherever applied, would make weight less
and work easier. I told her of many, many
ways in which the invention might be used,
and would have told her of many more if
she had not suddenly burst into tears.

"The world has gained something wonderful," she exclaimed, between her sobs, "but
I have lost a husband !"

"What do you mean by that ?" I asked,
in surprise.

"I haven't minded it so far," she said,
"because it gave you something to do, and

it pleased you, and it never interfered with our home pleasures and our home life. But now that is all over. You will never be your own master again. It will succeed, I am sure, and you may make a great deal of money, but we don't need money. What we need is the happiness which we have always had until now. Now there will be companies, and patents, and lawsuits, and experiments, and people calling you a humbug, and other people saying they discovered it long ago, and all sorts of persons coming to see you, and you'll be obliged to go to all sorts of places, and you will be an altered man, and we shall never be happy again. Millions of money will not repay us for the happiness we have lost."

These words of my wife struck me with much force. Before I had called her my mind had begun to be filled and perplexed with ideas of what I ought to do now that the great invention was perfected. Until now the matter had not troubled me at all. Sometimes I had gone backward and sometimes forward, but, on the whole, I had always felt encouraged. I had taken great pleasure in the work, but I had never allowed myself to be too much absorbed by it. But now everything was different. I

E. M.   F

began to feel that it was due to myself
and to my fellow-beings, that I should properly put this invention before the world.
And how should I set about it? What
steps should I take? I must make no mis-
takes.   When the matter should become
known hundreds of scientific people might
set themselves to work ; how could I tell but
that they might discover other methods of
producing the same effect? I must guard myself against a great many things.   I must get
patents in all parts of the world.   Already,
as I have said, my mind began to be troubled
and perplexed with these things.   A turmoil
of this sort did not suit my age or disposition.
I could not but agree with my wife that the
joys of a quiet and contented life were now
about to be broken into.

"My dear," said I, "I believe, with you,
that the thing will do us more harm than
good. If it were not for depriving the world
of the invention, I would throw the whole
thing to the winds.   And yet," I added,
regretfully, "I had expected a great deal of
personal gratification from the use of this
invention."

"Now, listen," said my wife eagerly,
"don't you think it would be best to do
this : use the thing as much as you please

for your own amusement and satisfaction, but let the world wait. It has waited a long time, and let it wait a little longer. When we are dead let Herbert have the invention. He will then be old enough to judge for himself whether it will be better to take advantage of it for his own profit, or simply to give it to the public for nothing. It would be cheating him if we were to do the latter, but it would also be doing him a great wrong if we were, at his age, to load him with such a heavy responsibility. Besides, if he took it up, you could not help going into it too."

I took my wife's advice. I wrote a careful and complete account of the invention, and, sealing it up, I gave it to my lawyers to be handed to my son after my death. If he died first, I would make other arrangements. Then I determined to get all the good and fun out of the thing that was possible without telling any one anything about it. Even Herbert, who was away from home, was not to be told of the invention.

The first thing I did was to buy a strong leathern knapsack, and inside of this I fastened my little machine, with a screw so arranged that it could be worked from the outside. Strapping this firmly to my shoulders, my wife gently turned the screw at the back until the upward tendency of the knapsack began to lift and sustain me. When I felt myself so gently supported and upheld that I seemed to weigh about thirty or forty pounds, I would set out for a walk. The knapsack did not raise me from the ground, but it gave me a very buoyant step. It was no labour at all to walk; it was a delight, an ecstasy. With the strength of a man and the weight of a child, I gaily strode along. The first day I walked half a dozen miles at a very brisk pace, and came back without feeling in the least degree tired. These walks now became one of the greatest joys of my life. When nobody was looking I would bound over a fence, sometimes just touching it with one hand, and sometimes not touching it at all. I delighted in rough places. I sprang over streams. I jumped and I ran. I felt like Mercury himself.

I now set about making another machine, so that my wife could accompany me in my walks; but when it was finished she positively refused to use it. "I can't wear a knapsack," she said, "and there is no other good way of fastening it to me. Besides, everybody about here knows I am no walker, and it would only set them talking."

I occasionally made use of this second machine, but I will only give one instance of its application. Some repairs were needed to the foundation-walls of my barn, and a two-horse wagon, loaded with building-stone, had been brought into my yard and left there. In the evening, when the men had gone away, I took my two machines and fastened them with strong chains, one on each side of the loaded wagon. Then, gradually turning the screws, the wagon was so lifted that its weight became very greatly diminished. We had an old donkey which used to belong to Herbert, and which was now occasionally used with a small cart to bring packages from the station. I went into the barn and put the harness on the little fellow, and, bringing him out to the wagon, I attached him to it. In this position he looked very funny, with a long pole sticking out in front of him and the great wagon behind him. When all was ready, I touched him up ; and, to my great delight, he moved off with the two-horse load of stone as easily as if he were drawing his own cart. I led him out into the public road, along which he proceeded without difficulty. He was an opinionated little beast, and sometimes stopped, not liking the peculiar manner in which he was harnessed; but a touch of the switch made him move on, and I soon turned him and brought the wagon back into the yard. This determined the success of my invention in one of its most important uses, and with a satisfied heart I put the donkey into the stable and went into the house.

Our trip to Europe was made a few months after this, and was mainly on our son Herbert's account. He, poor fellow, was in great trouble, and so, therefore, were we. He had become engaged, with our full consent, to a young lady in our town, the daughter of a gentleman whom we esteemed very highly. Herbert was young to be engaged to be married, but as we felt that he would never find a girl to make him so good a wife, we were entirely satisfied, especially as it was agreed on all hands that the marriage was not to take place for some time. It seemed to us that in marrying Janet Gilbert, Herbert would secure for himself, in the very beginning of his career, the most important element of a happy life. But suddenly, without any reason that seemed to us justifiable, Mr. Gilbert, the only surviving parent of Janet, broke off the match; and he and his daughter soon after left the town for a trip to the West.

This blow nearly broke poor Herbert's heart. He gave up his professional studies and came home to us, and for a time we thought he would be seriously ill. Then we took him to Europe, and after a Continental tour of a month or two we left him, at his own request, in Göttingen, where he thought it would do him good to go to work again. Then we went down to the little town in Italy where my story first finds us. My wife had suffered much in mind and body on her son's account, and for this reason I was anxious that she should take outdoor exercise, and enjoy as much as possible the bracing air of the country. I had brought with me both my little machines. One was still in my knapsack, and the other I had fastened to the inside of an enormous family trunk. As one is obliged to pay for nearly every pound of his baggage on the Continent, this saved me a great deal of money. Everything heavy was packed into this great trunk,—books, papers, the bronze, iron, and marble relics we had picked up, and all the articles that usually weigh down a tourist's baggage. I screwed up the negative gravity apparatus until the trunk could be handled with great ease by an ordinary porter. I could have made it weigh nothing at all,

but this, of course, I did not wish to do.
The lightness of my baggage, however, had
occasioned some comment, and I had over-
heard remarks which were not altogether
complimentary about people travelling
around with empty trunks; but this only
amused me.

Desirous that my wife should have the
advantage of negative gravity while taking
our walks, I had removed the machine from
the trunk and fastened it inside of the
basket, which she could carry under her
arm. This assisted her wonderfully. When
one arm was tired she put the basket under
the other, and thus, with one hand on my
arm, she could easily keep up with the free
and buoyant steps my knapsack enabled me
to take. She did not object to long tramps
here, because nobody knew that she was not
a walker, and she always carried some wine
or other refreshment in the basket, not only
because it was pleasant to have it with us,
but because it seemed ridiculous to go about
carrying an empty basket.

There were English-speaking people stopping at the hotel where we were, but they
seemed more fond of driving than walking,
and none of them offered to accompany us
on our rambles, for which we were very

glad. There was one man there, however, who was a great walker. He was an Englishman, a member of an Alpine Club, and generally went about dressed in a knickerbocker suit, with grey woollen stockings covering an enormous pair of calves. One evening this gentleman was talking to me and some others about the ascent of the Matterhorn, and I took occasion to deliver in pretty strong language my opinion upon such exploits. I declared them to be useless, foolhardy, and, if the climber had any one who loved him, wicked.

"Even if the weather should permit a view," I said, "what is that compared to the terrible risk to life? Under certain circumstances," I added (thinking of a kind of waistcoat I had some idea of making, which, set about with little negative gravity machines, all connected with a conveniently handled screw, would enable the wearer at times to dispense with his weight altogether), "such ascents might be divested of danger, and be quite admissible; but ordinarily they should be frowned upon by the intelligent public."

The Alpine Club man looked at me, especially regarding my somewhat slight figure and thinnish legs.

"It's all very well for you to talk that

way," he said, "because it is easy to see that you are not up to that sort of thing."

"In conversations of this kind," I replied, "I never make personal allusions; but since you have chosen to do so, I feel inclined to invite you to walk with me to-morrow to the top of the mountain to the north of this town."

"I'll do it," he said, "at any time you choose to name." And as I left the room soon afterward I heard him laugh.

The next afternoon, about two o'clock, the Alpine Club man and myself set out for the mountain.

"What have you got in your knapsack?" he said.

"A hammer, to use if I come across geological specimens, a field-glass, a flask of wine, and some other things."

"I wouldn't carry any weight, if I were you," he said.

"Oh, I don't mind it," I answered, and off we started.

The mountain to which we were bound was about two miles from the town. Its nearest side was steep, and in places almost precipitous, but it sloped away more gradually toward the north, and up that side a road led by devious windings to a village near the summit. It was not a very high mountain, but it would do for an afternoon's climb.

"I suppose you want to go up by the road," said my companion.

"Oh no," I answered, "we won't go so far around as that. There is a path up this side, along which I have seen men driving their goats. I prefer to take that."

"All right, if you say so," he answered, with a smile; "but you'll find it pretty tough."

After a time he remarked—

"I wouldn't walk so fast, if I were you."

"Oh, I like to step along briskly," I said. And briskly on we went.

My wife had screwed up the machine in the knapsack more than usual, and walking seemed scarcely any effort at all. I carried a long alpenstock, and when we reached the mountain and began the ascent, I found that with the help of this and my knapsack I could go uphill at a wonderful rate. My companion had taken the lead, so as to show me how to climb. Making a detour over some rocks, I quickly passed him and went ahead. After that it was impossible for him to keep up with me. I ran up steep places, I cut off the windings of the path by lightly clambering over rocks, and even when I followed the beaten track my step was as rapid as if I had been walking on level ground.

"Look here!" shouted the Alpine Club man from below, "you'll kill yourself if you go at that rate! That's no way to climb mountains."

"It's my way!" I cried. And on I skipped.

Twenty minutes after I arrived at the summit my companion joined me, puffing, and wiping his red face with his handkerchief.

"Confound it!" he cried, "I never came up a mountain so fast in my life."

"You need not have hurried," I said coolly.

"I was afraid something would happen to you," he growled, "and I wanted to stop you. I never saw a person climb in such an utterly absurd way."

"I don't see why you should call it absurd," I said, smiling with an air of superiority. "I arrived here in a perfectly comfortable condition, neither heated nor wearied."

He made no answer, but walked off to a little distance, fanning himself with his hat

and growling words which I did not catch.
After a time I proposed to descend.

"You must be careful as you go down,"
he said.   "It is much more dangerous to go
down steep places than to climb up."

"I am always prudent," I answered, and
started in advance.   I found the descent of
the mountain much more pleasant than the
ascent.   It was positively exhilarating.   I
jumped from rocks and bluffs eight and ten
feet in height, and touched the ground as
gently as if I had stepped down but two
feet.   I ran down steep paths, and, with
the aid of my alpenstock, stopped myself in
an instant.   I was careful to avoid dangerous places, but the runs and jumps I made
were such as no man had ever made before
upon that mountain-side.   Once only I heard
my companion's voice.

"You'll break your —— neck!" he yelled.

"Never fear!" I called back, and soon
left him far above.

When I reached the bottom I would have
waited for him, but my activity had warmed
me up, and as a cool evening breeze was beginning to blow I thought it better not to
stop and take cold.   Half an hour after my
arrival at the hotel I came down to the
court, cool, fresh, and dressed for dinner,

and just in time to meet the Alpine man as he entered, hot, dusty, and growling.

"Excuse me for not waiting for you," I said; but without stopping to hear my reason, he muttered something about waiting in a place where no one would care to stay, and passed into the house.

There was no doubt that what I had done gratified my pique and tickled my vanity.

"I think now," I said, when I related the matter to my wife, "that he will scarcely say that I am not up to that sort of thing."

"I am not sure," she answered, "that it was exactly fair. He did not know how you were assisted."

"It was fair enough," I said. "He is enabled to climb well by the inherited vigour of his constitution and by his training. He did not tell me what methods of exercise he used to get those great muscles upon his legs. I am enabled to climb by the exercise of my intellect. My method is my business and his method is his business. It is all perfectly fair."

Still she persisted—

"He *thought* that you climbed with your legs, and not with your head."

And now, after this long digression, necessary to explain how a middle-aged couple of slight pedestrian ability, and loaded with a heavy knapsack and basket, should have started out on a rough walk and climb, fourteen miles in all, we will return to ourselves, standing on the little bluff and gazing out upon the sunset view. When the sky began to fade a little we turned from it and prepared to go back to the town.

"Where is the basket?" I said.

"I left it right here," answered my wife. "I unscrewed the machine and it lay perfectly flat."

"Did you afterward take out the bottles?" I asked, seeing them lying on the grass.

"Yes, I believe I did. I had to take out yours in order to get at mine."

"Then," said I, after looking all about the grassy patch on which we stood, "I am afraid you did not entirely unscrew the instrument, and that when the weight of the bottles was removed the basket gently rose into the air."

"It may be so," she said lugubriously. "The basket was behind me as I drank my wine."

"I believe that is just what has happened," I said. "Look up there! I vow that is our basket!"

I pulled out my field-glass and directed it

at a little speck high above our heads. It was the basket floating high in the air. I gave the glass to my wife to look, but she did not want to use it.

"What shall I do?" she cried. "I can't walk home without that basket. It's perfectly dreadful!" And she looked as if she was going to cry.

"Do not distress yourself," I said, although I was a good deal disturbed myself. "We shall get home very well. You shall put your hand on my shoulder, while I put my arm around you. Then you can screw up my machine a good deal higher, and it will support us both. In this way I am sure that we shall get on very well."

We carried out this plan, and managed to walk on with moderate comfort. To be sure, with the knapsack pulling me upward, and the weight of my wife pulling me down, the straps hurt me somewhat, which they had not done before. We did not spring lightly over the wall into the road, but, still clinging to each other, we clambered awkwardly over it. The road for the most part declined gently toward the town, and with moderate ease we made our way along it. But we walked much more slowly than we had done before, and it was quite dark when we reached our hotel. If it had not been for the light inside the court it would have been difficult for us to find it. A travelling-carriage was standing before the entrance, and against the light. It was necessary to pass around it, and my wife went first. I attempted to follow her, but, strange to say, there was nothing under my feet. I stepped vigorously, but only wagged my legs in the air. To my horror I found that I was rising in the air! I soon saw, by the light below me, that I was some fifteen feet from the ground. The carriage drove away, and in the darkness I was not noticed. Of course I knew what had happened. The instrument in my knapsack had been screwed up to such an intensity, in order to support both myself and my wife, that when her weight was removed the force of the negative gravity was sufficient to raise me from the ground. But I was glad to find that when I had risen to the height I have mentioned I did not go up any higher, but hung in the air, about on a level with the second tier of windows of the hotel.

I now began to try to reach the screw in my knapsack in order to reduce the force of the negative gravity ; but, do what I would, I could not get my hand to it. The machine in the knapsack had been placed so as to support me in a well-balanced and comfortable way; and in doing this it had been impossible to set the screw so that I could reach it. But in a temporary arrangement of the kind this had not been considered necessary, as my wife always turned the screw for me until sufficient lifting-power had been attained. I had intended, as I have said before, to construct a negative gravity waistcoat, in which the screw should be in front, and entirely under the wearer's control; but this was a thing of the future.

When I found that I could not turn the screw I began to be much alarmed. Here I was, dangling in the air, without any means of reaching the ground. I could not expect my wife to return to look for me, as she would naturally suppose I had stopped to speak to some one. I thought of loosening myself from the knapsack, but this would not do, for I should fall heavily, and either kill myself or break some of my bones. I did not dare to call for assistance, for if any of the simple-minded inhabitants of the town had discovered me floating in the air they would have taken me for a demon, and would probably have shot at me. A moderate breeze was blowing, and it wafted me gently down the street. If it had blown me against a tree I would have seized it, and have endeavoured, so to speak, to climb down it; but there were no trees. There was a dim street lamp here and there, but reflectors above them threw their light upon the pavement, and none up to me. On many accounts I was glad that the night was so dark, for, much as I desired to get down, I wanted no one to see me in my strange position, which, to any one but myself and wife, would be utterly unaccountable. If I could rise as high as the roofs I might get on one of them, and, tearing off an armful of tiles, so load myself that I would be heavy enough to descend. But I did not rise to the eaves of any of the houses. If there had been a telegraph-pole, or anything of the kind that I could have clung to, I would have taken off the knapsack, and would have endeavoured to scramble down as well as I could. But there was nothing I could cling to. Even the water-spouts, if I could have reached the face of the houses, were embedded in the walls. At an open window, near which I was slowly blown, I saw two little boys going to bed by the light of a dim candle. I was dreadfully afraid that they would see me and raise an

alarm.   I actually came so near to the
window that I threw out one foot and
pushed against the wall with such force
that I went nearly across the street.   I
thought I caught sight of a frightened look
on the face of one of the boys; but of this
I am not sure, and I heard no cries.   I
still floated, dangling, down the street.
What was to be done?   Should I call out?
In that case, if I were not shot or stoned,
my strange predicament, and the secret of
my invention, would be exposed to the
world.   If I did not do this I must either
let myself drop and be killed or mangled,
or hang there and die.   When, during
the course of the night, the air became
more rarefied, I might rise higher and
higher, perhaps to an altitude of one or
two hundred feet.   It would then be impossible for the people to reach me and get
me down, even if they were convinced that
I was not a demon.   I should then expire,
and when the birds of the air had eaten all
of me that they could devour, I should for
ever hang above the unlucky town, a dangling skeleton, with a knapsack on its back.

Such thoughts were not reassuring, and
I determined that if I could find no means
of getting down without assistance, I would

call out and run all risks ; but so long as I could endure the tension of the straps I would hold out and hope for a tree or a pole.   Perhaps it might rain, and my wet clothes would then become so heavy that I would descend as low as the top of a lamp-post.

As this thought was passing through my mind I saw a spark of light upon the street approaching me.   I rightly imagined that it came from a tobacco-pipe, and presently I heard a voice.   It was that of the Alpine Club man.   Of all people in the world I did not want him to discover me, and I hung as motionless as possible.   The man was speaking to another person who was walking with him.

"He is crazy beyond a doubt," said the Alpine man.   "Nobody but a maniac could have gone up and down that mountain as he did !   He hasn't any muscles, and one need only look at him to know that he couldn't do any climbing in a natural way. It is only the excitement of insanity that gives him strength."

The two now stopped almost under me, and the speaker continued—

"Such things are very common with maniacs.   At times they acquire an un-

natural strength which is perfectly wonderful. I have seen a little fellow struggle and
fight so that four strong men could not hold
him."

Then the other person spoke—

"I am afraid what you say is too true,"
he remarked. "Indeed, I have known it for
some time."

At these words my breath almost stopped.
It was the voice of Mr. Gilbert, my towns-
man, and the father of Janet. It must have
been he who had arrived in the travelling-carriage. He was acquainted with the Alpine
Club man, and they were talking of me.
Proper or improper, I listened with all my
ears.

"It is a very sad case," Mr. Gilbert continued. "My daughter was engaged to
marry his son, but I broke off the match.
I could not have her marry the son of a
lunatic, and there could be no doubt of his
condition. He has been seen—a man of his
age, and the head of a family—to load himself up with a heavy knapsack, which there
was no earthly necessity for him to carry,
and go skipping along the road for miles,
vaulting over fences and jumping over rocks
and ditches like a young calf or colt. I myself saw a most heartrending instance of

how a kindly man's nature can be changed
by the derangement of his intellect. I
was at some distance from his house, but
I plainly saw him harness a little donkey
which he owns to a large two-horse wagon
loaded with stone, and beat and lash the
poor little beast until it drew the heavy
load some distance along the public road.
I would have remonstrated with him on this
horrible cruelty, but he had the wagon back
in his yard before I could reach him."

"Oh, there can be no doubt of his insanity," said the Alpine Club man, "and
he oughtn't to be allowed to travel about
in this way. Some day he will pitch his
wife over a precipice just for the fun of
seeing her shoot through the air."

"I am sorry he is here," said Mr. Gilbert, "for it would be very painful to meet
him. My daughter and I will retire very
soon, and go away as early to-morrow
morning as possible, so as to avoid seeing
him."

And then they walked back to the hotel.

For a few moments I hung, utterly forget-
ful of my condition, and absorbed in the consideration of these revelations. One idea
now filled my mind. Everything must be
explained to Mr. Gilbert, even if it should

be necessary to have him called to me, and
for me to speak to him from the upper
air.

Just then I saw something white appoach-
ing me along the road. My eyes had become accustomed to the darkness, and I
perceived that it was an upturned face. I
recognised the hurried gait, the form; it
was my wife. As she came near me I called
her name, and in the same breath entreated
her not to scream. It must have been an
effort for her to restrain herself, but she did
it.

"You must help me to get down," I said,
"without anybody seeing us."

"What shall I do?" she whispered.

"Try to catch hold of this string."

Taking a piece of twine from my pocket,
I lowered one end to her. But it was too
short; she could not reach it. I then tied
my handkerchief to it, but still it was not
long enough.

"I can get more string, or handkerchiefs,"
she whispered hurriedly.

"No," I said; "you could not get them up
to me. But, leaning against the hotel wall,
on this side, in the corner, just inside of the
garden gate, are some fishing-poles. I have
seen them there every day. You can easily

find them in the dark. Go, please, and bring
me one of those."

The hotel was not far away, and in a few
minutes my wife returned with a fishing-
pole. She stood on tiptoe, and reached it
high in air ; but all she could do was to
strike my feet and legs with it. My most
frantic exertions did not enable me to get
my hands low enough to touch it.

" Wait a minute," she said ; and the rod
was withdrawn.

I knew what she was doing. There was
a hook and line attached to the pole, and
with womanly dexterity she was fastening
the hook to the extreme end of the rod.
Soon she reached up, and gently struck at
my legs.   After a few attempts the hook
caught in my trousers, a little below my
right knee.   Then there was a slight pull,
a long scratch down my leg, and the hook
was stopped by the top of my boot.   Then
came a steady downward pull, and I felt
myself descending. Gently and firmly the
rod was drawn down ; carefully the lower
end was kept free from the ground ; and in
a few moments my ankle was seized with a
vigorous grasp.   Then some one seemed to
climb up me, my feet touched the ground,
an arm was thrown around my neck, the

hand of another arm was busy at the back
of my knapsack, and I soon stood firmly
in the road, entirely divested of negative
gravity.

"Oh that I should have forgotten,"
sobbed my wife, "and that I should have
dropped your arms, and let you go up into
the air! At first I thought that you had
stopped below, and it was only a little
while ago that the truth flashed upon me.
Then I rushed out and began looking up for
you. I knew that you had wax matches in
your pocket, and hoped that you would
keep on striking them, so that you would
be seen."

"But I did not wish to be seen," I said,
as we hurried to the hotel; "and I can
never be sufficiently thankful that it was
you who found me and brought me down.
Do you know that it is Mr. Gilbert and his
daughter who have just arrived? I must
see him instantly. I will explain it all to
you when I come upstairs."

I took off my knapsack and gave it to my
wife, who carried it to our room, while I
went to look for Mr. Gilbert. Fortunately
I found him just as he was about to go up
to his chamber. He took my offered hand,
but looked at me sadly and gravely.

"Mr. Gilbert," I said, "I must speak to you in private. Let us step into this room. There is no one here."

"My friend," said Mr. Gilbert, "it will be much better to avoid discussing this subject. It is very painful to both of us, and no good can come from talking of it."

"You cannot now comprehend what it is I want to say to you," I replied. "Come in here, and in a few minutes you will be very glad that you listened to me."

My manner was so earnest and impressive that Mr. Gilbert was constrained to follow me, and we went into a small room called the smoking-room, but in which people seldom smoked, and closed the door. I immediately began my statement. I told my old friend that I had discovered, by means that I need not explain at present, that he had considered me crazy, and that now the most important object of my life was to set myself right in his eyes. I thereupon gave him the whole history of my invention, and explained the reason of the actions that had appeared to him those of a lunatic. I said nothing about the little incident of that evening. That was a mere accident, and I did not care now to speak of it.

Mr. Gilbert listened to me very attentively.

" Your wife is here ?" he asked, when I had finished.

"Yes," I said; "and she will corroborate my story in every item, and no one could ever suspect her of being crazy. I will go and bring her to you."

In a few minutes my wife was in the room, had shaken hands with Mr. Gilbert, and had been told of my suspected madness. She turned pale, but smiled.

" He did act like a crazy man," she said, " but I never supposed that anybody would think him one." And tears came into her eyes.

" And now, my dear," said I, " perhaps you will tell Mr. Gilbert how I did all this."

And then she told him the story that I had told.

Mr. Gilbert looked from the one to the other of us with a troubled air.

"Of course I do not doubt either of you, or rather, I do not doubt that you believe what you say. All would be right if I could bring myself to credit that such a force as that you speak of can possibly exist."

"That is a matter," said I, "which I can

easily prove to you by actual demonstration. If you can wait a short time, until my wife and I have had something to eat,—for I am nearly famished, and I am sure she must be, —I will set your mind at rest upon that point."

"I will wait here," said Mr. Gilbert, "and smoke a cigar. Don't hurry yourselves. I shall be glad to have some time to think about what you have told me."

When we had finished the dinner, which had been set aside for us, I went upstairs and got my knapsack, and we both joined Mr. Gilbert in the smoking-room. I showed him the little machine, and explained, very briefly, the principle of its construction. I did not give any practical demonstration of its action, because there were people walking about the corridor who might at any moment come into the room ; but, looking out of the window, I saw that the night was much clearer. The wind had dissipated the clouds, and the stars were shining brightly.

"If you will come up the street with me," said I to Mr. Gilbert, "I will show you how this thing works."

"That is just what I·want to see," he answered.

"I will go with you," said my wife,

throwing a shawl over her head. And we started up the street.

When we were outside the little town I found the starlight was quite sufficient for my purpose. The white roadway, the low walls, and objects about us, could easily be distinguished.

"Now," said I to Mr. Gilbert, "I want to put this knapsack on you, and let you see how it feels, and how it will help you to walk." To this he assented with some eagerness, and I strapped it firmly on him. "I will now turn this screw," said I, "until you shall become lighter and lighter."

"Be very careful not to turn it too much," said my wife earnestly.

"Oh, you may depend on me for that," said I, turning the screw very gradually.

Mr. Gilbert was a stout man, and I was obliged to give the screw a good many turns.

"There seems to be considerable hoist in it," he said directly. And then I put my arms around him, and found that I could raise him from the ground. "Are you lifting me?" he exclaimed in surprise.

"Yes; I did it with ease," I answered.

"Upon — my — word!" ejaculated Mr. Gilbert.

I then gave the screw a half-turn more, and told him to walk and run. He started off, at first slowly, then he made long strides, then he began to run, and then to skip and jump. It had been many years since Mr. Gilbert had skipped and jumped. No one was in sight, and he was free to gambol as much as he pleased. "Could you give it another turn?" said he, bounding up to me. "I want to try that wall." I put on a little more negative gravity, and he vaulted over a five-foot wall with great ease. In an instant he had leaped back into the road, and in two bounds was at my side. "I came down as light as a cat," he said. "There was never anything like it." And away he went up the road, taking steps at least eight feet long, leaving my wife and me laughing heartily at the preternatural agility of our stout friend. In a few minutes he was with us again. "Take it off," he said. "If I wear it any longer I shall want one myself, and then I shall be taken for a crazy man, and perhaps clapped into an asylum."

"Now," said I, as I turned back the screw before unstrapping the knapsack, "do you understand how I took long walks, and leaped and jumped; how I ran uphill and downhill, and how the little donkey drew the loaded wagon?"

"I understand it all," cried he.   "I take back all I ever said or thought about you, my friend."

"And Herbert may marry Janet?" cried my wife.

"*May* marry her!" cried Mr. Gilbert. "Indeed he *shall* marry her, if I have anything to say about it!   My poor girl has been drooping ever since I told her it could not be."

My wife rushed at him, but whether she embraced him or only shook his hands I cannot say; for I had the knapsack in one hand, and was rubbing my eyes with the other.

"But, my dear fellow," said Mr. Gilbert directly, "if you still consider it to your interest to keep your invention a secret, I wish you had never made it. No one having a machine like that can help using it, and it is often quite as bad to be considered a maniac as to be one."

"My friend," I cried, with some excitement, "I have made up my mind on this subject. The little machine in this knapsack, which is the only one I now possess, has been a great pleasure to me. But I now know it has also been of the greatest injury indirectly to me and mine, not to mention some direct inconvenience and danger, which I will speak of another time. The secret lies with us three, and we will keep it. But the invention itself is too full of temptation and danger for any of us."

As I said this I held the knapsack with one hand while I quickly turned the screw with the other. In a few moments it was high above my head, while I with difficulty held it down by the straps. "Look!" I cried. And then I released my hold, and the knapsack shot into the air and disappeared into the upper gloom.

I was about to make a remark, but had no chance, for my wife threw herself upon my bosom, sobbing with joy.

"Oh, I am so glad—so glad!" she said. "And you will never make another?"

"Never another!" I answered.

"And now let us hurry in and see Janet," said my wife.

"You don't know how heavy and clumsy I feel," said Mr. Gilbert, striving to keep up with us as we walked back. "If I had worn that thing much longer, I should never have been willing to take it off!"

Janet had retired, but my wife went up to her room.

B. M.   H

" I think she has felt it as much as our boy," she said, when she rejoined me. "But I tell you, my dear, I left a very happy girl in that little bedchamber over the garden."

And there were three very happy elderly people talking together until quite late that evening. "I shall write to Herbert to-night," I said, when we separated, "and tell him to meet us all in Geneva. It will do the young man no harm if we interrupt his studies just now."

"You must let me add a postscript to the letter," said Mr. Gilbert, "and I am sure it will require no knapsack with a screw in the back to bring him quickly to us."

And it did not.

There is a wonderful pleasure in tripping over the earth like a winged Mercury, and in feeling one's-self relieved of much of that attraction of gravitation which drags us down to earth, and gradually makes the movement of our bodies but weariness and labour. But this pleasure is not to be compared, I think, to that given by the buoyancy and lightness of two young and loving hearts, reunited after a separation which they had supposed would last for ever.

What became of the basket and the knapsack, or whether they ever met in upper air,

I do not know.   If they but float away and stay away from ken of mortal man, I shall be satisfied.

And whether or not the world will ever know more of the power of negative gravity depends entirely upon the disposition of my son Herbert, when—after a good many years, I hope—he shall open the packet my lawyers have in keeping.

[NOTE.—It would be quite useless for any one to interview my wife on this subject, for she has entirely forgotten how my machine was made.   And as for Mr. Gilbert, he never knew.]

THE CHRISTMAS WRECK.

" WELL, sir," said old Silas, as he gave a preliminary puff to the pipe he had just lighted, and so satisfied himself that the draught was all right, "the wind's a-comin', an' so's Christmas. But it's no use bein' in a hurry fur either of 'em, fur sometimes they come afore you want 'em, anyway."

Silas was sitting in the stern of a small sailing-boat which he owned, and in which he sometimes took the Sandport visitors out for a sail ; and at other times applied to its more legitimate, but less profitable use, that of fishing. That afternoon he had taken young Mr. Nugent for a brief excursion on that portion of the Atlantic Ocean which sends its breakers up on the beach of Sandport. But he had found it difficult, nay, impossible just now, to bring him back, for the wind had gradually died away until there was not a breath of it left. Mr. Nugent, to whom nautical experiences were as new as the very nautical suit of blue flannel which he wore, rather liked the calm; it was such a relief to the monotony of rolling waves. He took out a cigar and lighted it, and then he remarked—

"I can easily imagine how a wind might come before you sailors might want it, but I don't see how Christmas could come too soon."

"It come wunst on me when things couldn't a looked more onready fur it," said Silas.

"How was that?" asked Mr. Nugent, settling himself a little more comfortably on the hard thwart. "If it's a story, let's have it. This is a good time to spin a yarn."

"Very well," said old Silas. "I'll spin her."

The bare-legged boy, whose duty it was to stay forward and mind the jib, came aft as soon as he smelt a story, and took a nautical position, which was duly studied by Mr. Nugent, on a bag of ballast in the bottom of the boat.

"It's nigh on to fifteen year ago," said Silas, "that I was on the barque, 'Mary Auguster,' bound for Sydney, New South Wales, with a cargo of canned goods. We was somewhere about longitood a hundred an' seventy, latitood nothin', an' it was the twenty-second o' December, when we was ketched by a reg'lar typhoon' which blew straight along, end on, fur a day an' a half. It blew away the storm sails; it blew away every yard, spar, shroud, an' every strand o' riggin', an' snapped the masts off, close to the deck; it blew away all the boats; it blew away the cook's caboose, an' everything else on deck; it blew off the hatches, an' sent 'em spinnin' in the air, about a mile to leeward; an' afore it got through, it washed away the cap'n an' all the crew 'cept me an' two others. These was Tom Simmons, the second mate, an' Andy Boyle, a chap from the Andirondack Mountins, who'd never been to sea afore. As he was a landsman he ought, by rights, to a been swep' off by the wind an' water, consid'rin' that the cap'n an' sixteen good seamen had gone a'ready. But he had hands eleven inches long, an' that give him a grip which no typhoon could git the better of. Andy had let out that his father was a miller up there in York State, an' a story had got round among the crew that his gran'father an' great gran'father was millers too; an' the way the fam'ly got such big hands come from

their habit of scoopin' up a extry quart or
two of meal or flour for themselves when they
was levellin' off their customers' measures.
He was a good-natered feller, though, an'
never got riled when I'd tell him to clap
his flour-scoops onter a halyard.

"We was all soaked, an' washed, an' beat,
an' battered. We held on some way or other
till the wind blowed itself out, an' then we
got on our legs an' began to look about us to
see how things stood. The sea had washed
into the open hatches till the vessel was
more'n half full of water, an' that had sunk
her so deep that she must 'a looked like a
canal boat loaded with gravel. We hadn't
had a thing to eat or drink durin' that whole
blow, an' we was pretty ravenous. We
found a keg of water which was all right,
and a box of biscuit, which was what you
might call soft tack, for they was soaked
through and through with sea-water. We
eat a lot of them so, fur we couldn't wait,
an' the rest we spread on the deck to dry,
fur the sun was now shinin' hot enough to
bake bread. We couldn't go below much,
fur there was a pretty good swell on the
sea, and things was floatin' about so's to
make it dangerous. But we fished out a
piece of canvas, which we rigged up agin

the stump of the main-mast so that we could have somethin' that we could sit down an' grumble under. What struck us all the hardest was that the barque was loaded with a whole cargo of jolly things to eat, which was just as good as ever they was, fur the water couldn't git through the tin cans in which they was all put up; an' here we was with nothin' to live on but them salted biscuit. There was no way of gittin' at any of the ship's stores, or any of the fancy prog, fur everythin' was stowed away tight under six or seven feet of water, an' pretty nigh all the room that was left between decks was filled up with extry spars, lumber, boxes, an' other floatin' stuff. All was shiftin', an' bumpin', an' bangin' every time the vessel rolled.

"As I said afore, Tom was second mate, an' I was bosen. Says I to Tom, 'The thing we've got to do is to put up some kind of a spar with a rag on it for a distress flag, so that we'll lose no time bein' took off.' 'There's no use a slavin' at anythin' like that,' says Tom, 'fur we've been blowed off the track of traders, an' the more we work the hungrier we'll git, an' the sooner will them biscuit be gone.'

"Now when I heerd Tom say this I sot

still, and began to consider. Being second
mate, Tom was, by rights, in command of
this craft; but it was easy enough to see
that if he commanded there'd never be
nothin' for Andy an' me to do. All the grit
he had in him he'd used up in holdin' on
durin' that typhoon. What he wanted to
do now was to make himself comfortable till
the time come for him to go to Davy Jones's
Locker; an' thinkin', most likely, that Davy
couldn't make it any hotter fur him than it
was on that deck, still in latitood nothin' at
all, fur we'd been blowed along the line
pretty nigh due West. So I calls to Andy,
who was busy turnin' over the biscuits on
the deck. 'Andy,' says I, when he had got
under the canvas, 'we's goin' to have a 'lec-
tion fur skipper. Tom here is about played
out. He's one candydate, an' I'm another.
Now, who do you vote fur? An', mind
yer eye, youngster, that you don't make no
mistake.' 'I vote fur you,' says Andy.
'Carried unanermous!' says I. 'An' I
want you to take notice that I'm cap'n of
what's left of the "Mary Auguster," an'
you two has got to keep your minds on that,
an' obey orders.' If Davy Jones was to do
all that Tom be Simmons said when he heard
this, the old chap would be kept busier

than he ever was yit. But I let him growl
his growl out, knowin' he'd come round all
right, fur there wasn't no help fur it, consid'rin' Andy an' me was two to his one.
Pretty soon we all went to work, an' got up
a spar from below which we rigged to the
stump of the foremast, with Andy's shirt
atop of it.

"Them sea-soaked, sun-dried biscuit was
pretty mean prog, as you might think, but
we eat so many of 'em that afternoon an'
'cordingly drank so much water that I was
obliged to put us all on short rations the
next day. 'This is the day before Christmas,' says Andy Boyle, 'an' to-night will be
Christmas Eve, an' it's pretty tough for us
to be sittin' here with not even so much hard
tack as we want, an' all the time thinkin'
that the hold of this ship is packed full
of the gayest kind of good things to eat.'
'Shut up about Christmas!' says Tom
Simmons. 'Them two youngsters of mine,
up in Bangor, is havin' their toes and noses
pretty nigh froze, I 'spect, but they'll
hang up their stockin's all the same to-
night, never thinkin' that their dad's bein'
cooked alive on a empty stomach.' 'Of
course they wouldn't hang 'em up,' says
I, 'if they knowed what a fix you was in,

but they don't know it, an' what's the use
of grumblin' at 'em for bein' a little jolly?'
'Well,' says Andy, 'they couldn't be more
jollier than I'd be if I could git at some of
them fancy fixin's down in the hold. I
worked well on to a week at 'Frisco puttin'
in them boxes, an' the names of the things
was on the outside of most of 'em, an' I tell
you what it is, mates, it made my mouth
water, even then, to read 'em, an' I wasn't
hungry nuther, havin' plenty to eat three
times a day. There was roast beef, an' roast
mutton, an' duck, an' chicken, an' soup, an'
peas, an' beans, an' termaters, an' plum-
puddin', an' mince-pie——' 'Shut up with
your mince-pie!' sung out Tom Simmons.
'Isn't it enough to have to gnaw on these
salt chips, without hearin' about mince-pie?'
'An' more 'n that,' says Andy, 'there was
canned peaches, an' pears, an' plums, an'
cherries.'

"Now these things did sound so cool an'
good to me on that broilin' deck, that I
couldn't stand it, an' I leans over to Andy,
an' I says : "Now look a here, if you don't
shut up talkin' about them things what's
stowed below, an' what we can't git at,
nohow, overboard you go!' 'That would
make you short-handed,' says Andy, with a

grin. 'Which is more'n you could say,' says I, 'if you'd chuck Tom an' me over'—alludin' to his eleven-inch grip. Andy didn't say no more then, but after a while he comes to me as I was lookin' round to see if anything was in sight, an' says he, 'I s'pose you ain't got nothin' to say agin my divin' into the hold just aft of the foremast, where there seems to be a bit of pretty clear water, an' see if I can't git up something?' 'You kin do it, if you like,' says I, 'but it's at your own risk. You can't take out no insurance at this office.' 'All right, then,' says Andy, 'an' if I git stove in by floatin' boxes, you an' Tom'll have to eat the rest of them salt crackers.' 'Now, boy,' says I —an' he wasn't much more, bein' only nineteen year old — 'you'd better keep out o' that hold. You'll just git yourself smashed. An' as to movin' any of them there heavy boxes, which must be swelled up as tight as if they was part of the ship, you might as well try to pull out one of the "Mary Auguster's" ribs.' 'I'll try it,' says Andy, 'fur to-morrer is Christmas, an' if I kin help it I ain't goin' to be floatin' atop of a Christmas dinner without eatin' any on it.' I let him go, fur he was a good swimmer and diver, an' I did hope he might root out

somethin' or other, fur Christmas is about
the worst day in the year fur men to be
starvin' on, and that's what we was a-
comin' to.

"Well, fur about two hours Andy swum,
an' dove, an' come up blubberin', an' dodged
all sorts of floatin' an' pitchin' stuff, fur the
swell was still on; but he couldn't even be so
much as sartain that he'd found the canned
vittles.   To dive down through hatchways,
an' among broken bulkheads, to hunt fur
any partiklar kind o' boxes under seven feet
of sea-water ain't no easy job; an' though
Andy says he got hold of the end of a box
that felt to him like the big 'uns he'd noticed
as havin' the meat pies in, he couldn't move
it no more'n if it had been the stump of the
foremast.   If we could have pumped the
water out of the hold we could have got at
any part of the cargo we wanted, but as it
was, we couldn't even reach the ship's stores,
which, of course, must have been mostly
spiled anyway; whereas the canned vittles
was just as good as new. The pumps was
all smashed, or stopped up, for we tried 'em,
but if they hadn't a been we three couldn't
never have pumped out that ship on three
biscuit a day, and only about two days'
rations at that.

"So Andy he come up, so fagged out that it was as much as he could do to get his clothes on, though they wasn't much, an' then he stretched himself out under the canvas an' went to sleep, an' it wasn't long afore he was talkin' about roast turkey an' cranberry sass, an' punkin pie, an' sech stuff, most of which we knowed was under our feet that present minute. Tom Simmons he just b'iled over, an' sung out: 'Roll him out in the sun and let him cook! I can't stand no more of this!' But I wasn't goin' to have Andy treated no sech way as that, fur if it hadn't been fur Tom Simmons' wife an' young uns, Andy'd been worth two of him to anybody who was consid'rin' savin' life. But I give the boy a good punch in the ribs to stop his dreamin', fur I was as hungry as Tom was, and couldn't stand no nonsense about Christmas dinners.

"It was a little arter noon when Andy woke up, an' he went outside to stretch himself. In about a minute he give a yell that made Tom and me jump. 'A sail!' he hollered, 'a sail!' An' you may bet your life, young man, that 'twasn't more'n half a second before us two had scuffled out from under that canvas, an' was standin' by Andy. 'There she is!' he shouted, 'not a mile to win'ard.' I give one look, an' then I sings out: ''Tain't a sail! It's a flag of distress! Can't you see, you land-lubber, that that's the stars and stripes up-side down?' 'Why, so it is,' said Andy, with a couple of reefs in the joyfulness of his voice. An' Tom, he began to growl as if somebody had cheated him out of half a year's wages.

"The flag that we saw was on the hull of a steamer that had been driftin' down on us while we was sittin' under our canvas. It was plain to see she'd been caught in the typhoon too, fur there wasn't a mast or a smoke-stack on her; but her hull was high enough out of the water to catch what wind there was, while we was so low-sunk that we didn't make no way at all. There was people aboard, and they saw us, an' waved their hats an' arms, an' Andy an' me waved ours, but all we could do was to wait till they drifted nearer, fur we hadn't no boats to go to 'em if we'd a wanted to.

"'I'd like to know what good that old hulk is to us,' said Tom Simmons. 'She can't take us off.' It did look to me some-thin' like the blind leadin' the blind; but Andy he sings out: 'We'd be better off

aboard of her, fur she ain't water-logged,
an', more'n that, I don't s'pose her stores
are all soaked up in salt water.' There was
some sense in that, and when the steamer
had got to within half a mile of us, we was
glad to see a boat put out from her with
three men in it. It was a queer boat, very
low an' flat, an' not like any ship's boat I
ever see. But the two fellers at the oars
pulled stiddy, an' pretty soon the boat was
'longside of us, an' the three men on our
deck. One of 'em was the first mate of the
other wreck, an' when he found out what
was the matter with us, he spun his yarn,
which was a longer one than ours. His
vessel was the 'Water Crescent,' nine hundred tons, from 'Frisco to Melbourne, and
they had sailed about six weeks afore we
did. They was about two weeks out when
some of their machinery broke down, an'
when they got it patched up it broke agin,
worse than afore, so that they couldn't do
nothin' with it. They kep' along under
sail for about a month, makin' mighty poor
headway till the typhoon struck 'em, an'
that cleaned their decks off about as slick
as it did ours, but their hatches wasn't
blowed off, an' they didn't ship no water
wuth mentionin', an' the crew havin' kep'

below, none on 'em was lost. But now they was clean out of provisions and water, havin' been short when the breakdown happened, fur they had sold all the stores they could spare to a French brig in distress that they overhauled when about a week out. When they sighted us they felt pretty sure they 'd git some provisions out of us. But when I told the mate what a fix we was in his jaw dropped till his face was as long as one of Andy's hands. Howsomdever he said he 'd send the boat back fur as many men as it could bring over, and see if they couldn't get up some of our stores. Even if they was soaked with salt water, they 'd be better than nothin'. Part of the cargo of the 'Water Crescent' was tools an' things fur some railway contractors out in Australier, an' the mate told the men to bring over some of them irons that might be used to fish out the stores. All their ship's boats had been blowed away, an' the one they had was a kind of shore boat for fresh water, that had been shipped as part of the cargo, an' stowed below. It couldn't stand no kind of a sea, but there wasn't nothin' but a swell on ; an' when it come back it had the cap'n in it, an' five men, besides a lot of chains an' tools.

" Them fellers an' us worked pretty nigh
the rest of the day, an' we got out a couple
of bar'ls of water, which was all right,
havin' been tight bunged ; an' a lot of sea
biscuit, all soaked an' sloppy, but we only
got a half bar'l of meat, though three or
four of the men stripped an' dove fur
more 'n an hour. We cut up some of the
meat, an' eat it raw, an the cap'n sent some
over to the other wreck, which had drifted
past us to leeward, an' would have gone
clean away from us if the cap'n hadn't had
a line got out an' made us fast to it while
we was a workin' at the stores.

" That night the cap'n took us three, as
well as the provisions we 'd got out, on
board his hull, where the 'commodations
was consid'able better than they was on the
half-sunk 'Mary Auguster.' An' afore we
turned in he took me aft, an' had a talk
with me as commandin' off'cer of my vessel.
' That wreck o' yourn,' says he, ' has got a
vallyble cargo in it, which isn't spiled by
bein' under water. Now, if you could get
that cargo into port it would put a lot of
money in your pocket, fur the owners
couldn't git out of payin' you fur takin'
charge of it, an' havin' it brung in. Now
I 'll tell you what I 'll do. I 'll lie by you,

an' I 've got carpenters aboard that 'll put
your pumps in order, an' I 'll set my men to
work to pump out your vessel. An' then,
when she 's afloat all right, I 'll go to work
agin at my vessel, which I didn't s'pose
there was any use o' doin'; but whilst I
was huntin' round amongst our cargo to-
day I found that some of the machinery we
carried might be worked up so 's to take
the place of what is broke in our engin'.
We 've got a forge aboard, an' I believe we
can make these pieces of machinery fit, an'
git goin' agin. Then I 'll tow you into
Sydney, an' we 'll divide the salvage money.
I won't git nothin' for savin' my vessel, coz
that 's my bizness; but you wasn't cap'n o'
yourn, an' took charge of her a purpose to
save her, which is another thing.'

"I wasn't at all sure that I didn't take
charge of the 'Mary Auguster' to save myself an' not the vessel, but I didn't mention
that, an' asked the cap'n how he expected
to live all this time. 'Oh, we kin git at
your stores easy enough,' says he, 'when
the water 's pumped out.' 'They 'll be
mostly spiled,' says I. 'That don't matter,'
says he, 'men 'll eat anythin', when they
can't git nothin' else.' An' with that he
left me to think it over.

"I must say, young man, an' you kin b'lieve me if you know anythin' about sech things, that the idee of a pile of money was mighty temptin' to a feller like me, who had a girl at home ready to marry him, and who would like nothin' better'n to have a little house of his own, an' a little vessel of his own, an' give up the other side of the world altogether. But while I was goin' over all this in my mind, an' wonderin' if the cap'n ever could git us into port, along comes Andy Boyle, and sits down beside me. 'It drives me pretty nigh crazy,' says he, 'to think that to-morrer's Christmas, an' we've got to feed on that sloppy stuff we fished out of our stores, an' not much of it nuther, while there's all that roast turkey, an' plum-puddin', an' mince-pie, a-floatin' out there just before our eyes, an' we can't have none of it.' 'You hadn't oughter think so much about eatin', Andy,' says I, 'but if I was talkin' about them things I wouldn't leave out canned peaches. By George! Of a hot Christmas like this is goin' to be, I'd be the jolliest Jack on the ocean if I could git at that canned fruit.' 'Well, there's a way,' says Andy, 'that we might git some of 'em. A part of the cargo of this ship is stuff for blastin' rocks; catridges, 'lectric bat'ries, an' that sort of thing ; an' there 's a man aboard who 's goin' out to take charge of 'em. I 've been talkin' to this bat'ry man, an' I 've made up my mind it 'll be easy enough to lower a little catridge down among our cargo, an' blow out a part of it.' 'What ud be the good of it,' says I, 'blowed into chips?' 'It might smash some,' he said, 'but others would be only loosened, an' they 'd float up to the top, where we could get 'em, 'specially them as was packed with pies, which must be pretty light.' 'Git out, Andy,' says I, 'with all that stuff !' An' he got out.

"But the idees he 'd put into my head didn't git out, an' as I laid on my back on the deck, lookin' up at the stars, they sometimes seemed to put themselves into the shape of little houses, with a little woman cookin' at the kitchin fire, an' a little schooner layin' at anchor just off shore ; an' then agin they 'd hump themselves up till they looked like a lot of new tin cans with their tops off, an' all kinds of good things to eat inside, 'specially canned peaches — the big white kind—soft an' cool, each one split in half, with a holler in the middle filled with juice. By George, sir, the very thought of a tin can like that made me beat my heels

agin the deck. I'd been mighty hungry, an'
had eat a lot of salt pork, wet an' raw, an'
now the very idee of it, even cooked, turned
my stomach. I looked up to the stars agin,
an' the little house an' the little schooner was
clean gone, an' the whole sky was filled with
nothin' but bright new tin cans.

"In the mornin', Andy, he come to me
agin. 'Have you made up your mind,' says
he, 'about gittin' some of them good things
for Christmas dinner?' 'Confound you!'
says I, 'you talk as if all we had to do was
to go an' git 'em.' 'An' that's what I b'lieve
we kin do,' says he, 'with the help of that
bat'ry man.' 'Yes,' says I, 'an' blow a lot
of the cargo into flinders, an' damage the
"Mary Auguster" so's she couldn't never
be took into port.' An' then I told him
what the cap'n had said to me, an' what I
was goin' to do with the money. 'A little
catridge,' says Andy, 'would do all we
want, an' wouldn't hurt the vessel nuther.
Besides that, I don't b'lieve what this cap'n
says about tinkerin' up his engin'. 'Tain't
likely he'll ever git her runnin' agin, nor
pump out the "Mary Auguster" nuther.
If I was you I'd a durned sight ruther have
a Christmas dinner in hand than a house an'
wife in the bush.' 'I ain't thinkin' o'

marryin' a girl in Australier,' says I. An'
Andy he grinned, an' said I wouldn't marry
nobody if I had to live on spiled vittles till
I got her.

"A little after that I went to the cap'n,
an' I told him about Andy's idee, but he
was down on it. 'It's your vessel, an' not
mine,' says he, 'an' if you want to try to
git a dinner out of her I'll not stand in your
way. But it's my 'pinion you'll just
damage the ship, an' do nothin'.' Howsomdever I talked to the bat'ry man about
it, an' he thought it could be done, an' not
hurt the ship nuther. The men was all in
favour of it, for none of 'em had forgot it
was Christmas day. But Tom Simmons, he
was agin it strong, for he was thinkin' he'd
git some of the money if we got the 'Mary
Auguster' into port. He was a selfish-
minded man, was Tom, but it was his
nater, an' I s'pose he couldn't help it.

"Well, it wasn't long afore I began to
feel pretty empty, an' mean, an' if I'd a
wanted any of the prog we got out the day
afore, I couldn't have found much, for the
men had eat it up nearly all in the night.
An' so, I just made up my mind without
any more foolin', an' me, and Andy Boyle,
an' the bat'ry man, with some catridges an'

a coil of wire, got into the little shore boat,
and pulled over to the 'Mary Auguster.'
There we lowered a small catridge down
the main hatchway, an' let it rest down
among the cargo. Then we rowed back to
the steamer, uncoilin' the wire as we went.
The bat'ry man clumb up on deck, an' fixed
his wire to a 'lectric machine, which he'd
got all ready afore we started. Andy and
me didn't git out of the boat; we had too
much sense for that, with all them hungry
fellers waitin' to jump in her; but we just
pushed a little off, an' sot waitin', with our
mouths a-waterin', for him to touch her off.
He seemed to be a long time about it, but
at last he did it, an' that instant there was
a bang on board the 'Mary Auguster' that
made my heart jump. Andy an' me pulled
fur her like mad, the others a hollerin' arter
us, an' we was on deck in no time. The
deck was all covered with the water that
had been throwed up; but I tell you, sir,
that we poked an' fished about, an' Andy
stripped an' went down, an' swum all round,
an' we couldn't find one floatin' box of
canned goods. There was a lot of splinters,
but where they come from we didn't know.
By this time my dander was up, an' I just
pitched around savage. That little catridge

wasn't no good, an' I didn't intend to stand
any more foolin'. We just rowed back to
the other wreck, an' I called to the bat'ry
man to come down, an' bring some bigger
catridges with him, fur if we was goin' to do
anythin' we might as well do it right. So
he got down with a package of bigger ones,
an' jumped into the boat. The cap'n he
called out to us to be keerful, an' Tom
Simmons leaned over the rail, an' swored,
but I didn't pay no 'tention to nuther of
'em, an' we pulled away.

"When I got aboard the 'Mary Augnster'
I says to the bat'ry man : 'We don't want
no nonsense this time, an' I want you to put
in enough catridges to heave up somethin'
that'll do fur a Christmas dinner. I don't
know how the cargo is stored, but you kin
put one big catridge 'midship, another for-
'ard, an' another aft, an' one or nuther of
'em oughter fetch up somethin'.' Well, we
got the three catridges into place. They
was a good deal bigger than the one we
first used, an' we j'ined 'em all to one wire,
an' then we rowed back, carryin' the long
wire with us. When we reached the
steamer, me an' Andy was a-goin' to stay
in the boat as we did afore, but the cap'n
sung out that he wouldn't allow the bat'ry

to be touched off till we come aboard. 'Ther's got to be fair play,' says he. 'It's your vittles, but it's my side that's doin' the work. After we've blasted her this time you two can go in the boat, an' see what there is to get hold of, but two of my men must go along.' So me an' Andy had to go on deck, an' two big fellers was detailed to go with us in the little boat when the time come ; an' then the bat'ry man, he teched her off.

"Well, sir, the pop that followed that tech was somethin' to remember. It shuck the water, it shuck the air, an' it shuck the hull we was on. A reg'lar cloud of smoke an' flyin' bits of things rose up out of the 'Mary Auguster.' An' when that smoke cleared away, an' the water was all bilin' with the splash of various-sized hunks that come rainin' down from the sky, what was left of the 'Mary Auguster' was sprinkled over the sea like a wooden carpet for water-birds to walk on.

"Some of the men sung out one thing, an' some another, an' I could hear Tom Simmons swear, but Andy an' me said never a word, but scuttled down into the boat, follered close by the two men who was to go with us. Then we rowed like devils for the lot of stuff that was bobbin' about on the water, out where the 'Mary Auguster' had been. In we went, among the floatin' spars and ship's timbers, I keepin' the things off with an oar, the two men rowin', an' Andy in the bow.

"Suddenly Andy give a yell, an' then he reached himself for'ard with sech a bounce that I thought he'd go overboard. But up he come in a minnit, his two 'leven-inch hands gripped round a box. He sot down in the bottom of the boat with the box on his lap, an' his eyes screwed on some letters that was stamped on one end. 'Pidjin pies!' he sings out. ''Tain't turkeys, nor 'tain't cranberries. But, by the Lord Harry, it's Christmas pies all the same!' After that Andy didn't do no more work, but sot holdin' that box as if it had been his fust baby. But we kep' pushin' on to see what else there was. It's my 'pinion that the biggest part of the bark's cargo was blowed into mince-meat, an' the most of the rest of it was so heavy that it sunk. But it wasn't all busted up, an' it didn't all sink. There was a big piece of wreck with a lot of boxes stove into the timbers, and some of these had in 'em beef ready biled an' packed into cans, an' there was other kinds of meat, an' dif'rent sorts of vegetables, an' one box of turtle soup. I looked at every one of 'em as we took 'em in, an' when we got the little boat pretty well loaded I wanted to still keep on searchin', but the men, they said that shore boat ud sink if we took in any more cargo, an' so we put back, I feelin' glummer'n I oughter felt, fur I had begun to be afeared that canned fruit, such as peaches, was heavy, an' li'ble to sink.

"As soon as we had got our boxes aboard, four fresh men put out in the boat, an' after awhile they come back with another load; an' I was mighty keerful to read the names on all the boxes. Some was meat pies, an' some was salmon, an' some was potted herrin's, an' some was lobsters. But nary a thing could I see that ever had growed on a tree.

"Well, sir, there was three loads brought in altogether, an' the Christmas dinner we had on the for'ard deck of that steamer's hull was about the jolliest one that was ever seen of a hot day aboard of a wreck in the Pacific Ocean. The cap'n kept good order, an' when all was ready the tops was jerked off the boxes, and each man grabbed a can an' opened it with his knife. When he had cleaned it out, he tuk another without

doin' much questionin' as to the bill of fare.
Whether anybody got pidjin pie 'cept Andy,
I can't say, but the way we piled in Del-
moniker prog would a made people open
their eyes as was eatin' their Christmas
dinners on shore that day. Some of the
things would a been better, cooked a little
more, or het up, but we was too fearful
hungry to wait for that, an' they was tip-
top as they was.

"The cap'n went out afterwards, an' towed
in a couple of bar'ls of flour that was only
part soaked through, an' he got some other
plain prog that would do fur futur use; but
none of us give our minds to stuff like this
arter the glorious Christmas dinner that
we'd quarried out of the 'Mary Auguster.'
Every man that wasn't on duty went below,
and turned in for a snooze. All 'cept me,
an' I didn't feel just altogether satisfied.
To be sure I'd had an A 1 dinner, an'
though a little mixed, I'd never eat a jollier
one on any Christmas that I kin look back
at. But, fur all that, there was a hanker
inside o' me. I hadn't got all I'd laid out to
git, when we teched off the 'Mary Auguster.'
The day was blazin' hot, an' a lot of the
things I'd eat was pretty peppery. 'Now,'
thinks I, 'if there had a been just one can

o' peaches sech as I see shinin' in the stars last night,' an' just then, as I was walkin' aft, all by myself, I seed lodged on the stump of the mizzenmast, a box with one corner druv down among the splinters. It was half split open, an' I could see the tin cans shinin' through the crack. I give one jump at it, an' wrenched the side off. On the top of the first can I seed was a picture of a big white peach with green leaves. That box had been blowed up so high that if it had come down anywhere 'cept among them splinters it would a smashed itself to flinders, or killed somebody. So fur as I know, it was the only thing that fell nigh us, an' by George, sir, I got it ! When I had finished a can of 'em I hunted up Andy, an' then we went aft, an' eat some more. ' Well,' says Andy, as we was a-eatin', ' how d'ye feel now about blowin' up your wife, an' your house, an' that little schooner you was goin' to own ? '

" ' Andy,' says I, ' this is the joyfulest Christmas I 've had yit, an' if I was to live till twenty hundred I don't b'lieve I 'd have no joyfuler, with things comin' in so pat, so don't you throw no shadders.'

" ' Shadders,' says Andy, ' that ain't me. I leave that sort of thing fur Tom Simmons.'

B. M.   K

" ' Shadders is cool,' says I, ' an' I kin go to sleep under all he throws.'

" Well, sir," continued old Silas, putting his hand on the tiller and turning his face seaward, "if Tom Simmons had kept command of that wreck, we all would a laid there an' waited an' waited till some of us was starved, an' the others got nothin' fur it, fur the cap'n never mended his engin', an' it was more'n a week afore we was took off, an' then it was by a sailin' vessel, which left the hull of the 'Water Crescent' behind her, just as she would a had to leave the 'Mary Auguster' if that jolly old Christmas wreck had a been there.

" An' now, sir," said Silas, "d'ye see that stretch o' little ripples over yander, lookin' as if it was a lot o' herrin' turnin' over to dry their sides? Do you know what that is? That 's the supper wind. That means coffee, an' hot cakes, an' a bit of br'iled fish, an' pertaters, an' p'raps—if the old woman feels in a partiklar good humour — some canned peaches, big white uns, cut in half, with a holler place in the middle filled with cool, sweet juice."

OUR ARCHERY CLUB.

WHEN an archery club was formed in our village, I was among the first to join it; but I should not, on this account, claim any extraordinary enthusiasm on the subject of archery, for nearly all the ladies and gentlemen of the place were also among the first to join.

Few of us, I think, had a correct idea of the popularity of archery in our midst, until the subject of a club was broached. Then we all perceived what a strong interest we felt in the study and use of the bow and arrow. The club was formed immediately; and our thirty members began to discuss the relative merits of lancewood, yew, and green-heart bows, and to survey yards and lawns for suitable spots for setting up targets for home practice.

Our weekly meetings, at which we came together to show in friendly contest how much our home practice had taught us, were held upon the village green, or rather upon what had been intended to be the village green. This pretty piece of ground, partly in smooth lawn, and partly shaded by fine trees, was the property of a gentleman of the place, who had presented it, under certain conditions, to the township. But as the township had never fulfilled any of the conditions, and had done nothing toward the improvement of the spot, further than to make it a grazing-place for local cows and goats, the owner had withdrawn his gift, shut out the cows and goats by a picket-fence, and having locked the gate, had hung up the key in his barn. When our club was formed, the green, as it was still called, was offered to us for our meetings; and with proper gratitude, we elected its owner to be our president.

This gentleman was eminently qualified for the presidency of an archery club. In the first place, he did not shoot: this gave him time and opportunity to attend to the shooting of others. He was a tall and pleasant man, a little elderly. This "elderliness," if I may so put it, seemed, in his case, to resemble some mild disorder, like a gentle rheumatism, which, while it prevented him from indulging in all the wild hilarities of youth, gave him, in compensation, a position, as one entitled to a certain consideration, which was very agreeable to him. His little disease was chronic, it is true, and it was growing upon him ; but it was, so far, a pleasant ailment.

And so, with as much interest in bows, and arrows, and targets, and successful shots as any of us, he never fitted an arrow to a string, nor drew a bow ; but he attended every meeting, settling disputed points (for he studied all the books on archery) ; encouraging the disheartened ; holding back the eager ones, who would run to the targets as soon as they had shot, regardless of the fact that others were still shooting, and that the human body is not arrow-proof ; and shedding about him that general aid and comfort which emanates from a good fellow, no matter what he may say or do.

There were persons—outsiders—who said that archery clubs always selected ladies for their presiding officers, but we did not care to be too much bound down and trammelled by customs and traditions. Another club might not have among its members such a genial, elderly gentleman, who owned a village green.

I soon found myself greatly interested in archery, especially when I succeeded in planting an arrow somewhere within the periphery of the target ; but I never became such an enthusiast in bow-shooting as my friend Pepton.

If Pepton could have arranged matters to suit himself, he would have been born an archer ; but as this did not happen to have been the case, he employed every means in his power to rectify what he considered this serious error in his construction. He gave his whole soul, and the greater part of his spare time, to archery ; and as he was a young man of energy, this helped him along wonderfully.

His equipments were perfect : no one could excel him in this respect. His bow was snake-wood, backed with hickory. He carefully rubbed it down every evening with oil and beeswax, and it took its repose in a green baize bag. His arrows were Philip Highfield's best ; his strings the finest Flanders hemp. He had shooting-gloves ; and he had little leathern tips, that could be screwed fast on the ends of what he called his string-fingers. He had a quiver and a belt ; and when equipped for the weekly meetings, he carried a fancy-coloured wiping-tassel, and a little ebony grease-pot, hanging from his belt. He wore, when shooting, a polished arm-guard or bracer; and if he had heard of anything else that an archer should have, he straightway would have procured it.

Pepton was a single man; and he lived with two good old maiden ladies, who took as much care of him as if they had been his mothers. And he was such a good, kind fellow that he deserved all the attention they gave him. They felt a great interest in his archery pursuits, and shared his anxious solicitude in the selection of a suitable place to hang his bow.

"You see," said he, "a fine bow like this, when not in use, should always be in a perfectly dry place."

"And when in use too," said Miss Martha; "for I am sure that you oughtn't to be standing and shooting in any damp spot. There's no surer way of gettin' chilled."

To which sentiment Miss Maria agreed, and suggested wearing rubber shoes, or having a board to stand on, when the club met after a rain.

Pepton first hung his bow in the hall; but after he had arranged it symmetrically upon two long nails (bound with green worsted, lest they should scratch the bow

through its woollen cover), he reflected that
the front door would frequently be open,
and that damp draughts must often go
through the hall.   He was sorry to give up
this place for his bow, for it was convenient
and appropriate; and for an instant he
thought that it might remain, if the front
door could be kept shut, and visitors admitted through a little side door, which the
family generally used, and which was almost as convenient as the other,—except,
indeed, on wash-days, when a wet sheet or
some article of wearing apparel was apt to
be hung in front of it.   But, although wash-
day occurred but once a week, and although
it was comparatively easy, after a little practice, to bob under a high-propped sheet,
Pepton's heart was too kind to allow his
mind to dwell upon this plan.   So he drew
the nails from the wall of the hall, and put
them up in various places about the house.
His own room had to be aired a great deal
in all weathers, and so that would not do
at all.   The wall above the kitchen fire-
place would be a good location, for the
chimney was nearly always warm; but
Pepton could not bring himself to keep his
bow in the kitchen : there would be nothing
æsthetic about such a disposition of it; and,

besides, the girl might be tempted to string and bend it. The old ladies really did not want it in the parlour, for its length and its green baize cover would make it an encroaching and unbecoming neighbour to the little engravings and the big samplers, the picture-frames of acorns and pine-cones, the fancifully patterned ornaments of clean wheat-straw, and all the quaint adornments which had hung upon those walls for so many years. But they did not say so. If it had been necessary, to make room for the bow they would have taken down the pencilled profiles of their grandfather, their grandmother, and their father when a little boy, which hung in a row over the mantel-piece.

However, Pepton did not ask this sacrifice. In the summer evenings the parlour windows must be open. The dining-room was really very little used in the evening, except when Miss Maria had stockings to darn; and then she always sat in that apartment, and of course she had the windows open. But Miss Maria was very willing to bring her work into the parlour, —it was foolish, any way, to have a feeling about darning stockings before chance company,—and then the dining-room could be kept shut up after tea. So into the wall of that neat little room Pepton drove his worsted-covered nails, and on them carefully laid his bow. And the next day Miss Martha and Miss Maria went about the house, and covered the nail-holes he had made with bits of wall-paper, carefully snipped out to fit the patterns, and pasted on so neatly that no one would have suspected they were there.

One afternoon, as I was passing the old ladies' house, I saw, or thought I saw, two men carrying in a coffin. I was struck with alarm.

"What !" I thought, "can either of those good women——? Or, can Pepton——?"

Without a moment's hesitation I rushed in behind the men. There, at the foot of the stairs, directing them, stood Pepton. Then it was not he ! I seized him sympathetically by the hand.

"Which——?" I faltered. "Which? Who is that coffin for ?"

"Coffin !" cried Pepton, "why, my dear fellow, that is not a coffin. That is my ascham."

"Ascham ?" I exclaimed. "What is that ?"

"Come and look at it," he said, when the

men had set it on end against the wall; "it
is an upright closet, or receptacle for an
archer's armament.   Here is a place to
stand the bow; here are supports for the
arrows and quivers; here are shelves and
hooks, on which to lay or hang everything
the merry man can need.   And you see,
moreover, that it is lined with green plush,
and that the door fits tightly, so that it can
stand anywhere, and there need be no fear of
draughts or damps affecting my bow.   Isn't
it a perfect thing?   You ought to get one."

I admitted the perfection, but agreed no
further.   I had not the income of my good
Pepton.

Pepton was, indeed, most wonderfully
well equipped, and yet, little did those dear
old ladies think, when they carefully dusted
and reverentially gazed at the bunches of
arrows, the arm-bracers, the gloves, the
grease-pots, and all the rest of the para-
phernalia of archery, as it hung around
Pepton's room; or when they afterward
allowed a particular friend to peep at it, all
arranged so orderly within the ascham; or
when they looked with sympathetic, loving
admiration on the beautiful polished bow,
when it was taken out of its bag,—little did
they think, I say, that Pepton was the very

poorest shot in the club. In all the surface
of the much perforated targets of the club,
there was scarcely a hole that he could put
his hand upon his heart and say he made.

Indeed, I think it was the truth that
Pepton was born not to be an archer. There
were young fellows in the club, who shot
with bows that cost no more than Pepton's
tassels, but who could stand up and whang
arrows into the targets all the afternoon, if
they could get a chance; and there were
ladies who made hits five times out of six;
and there were also all the grades of archers
common to any club. But there was no one
but himself in Pepton's grade. He stood
alone, and it was never any trouble to add
up his score.

And yet he was not discouraged. He
practised every day except Sundays, and
indeed he was the only person in the club
who practised at night. When he told me
about this, I was a little surprised.

"Why, it's easy enough," said he. "You
see, I hung a lantern, with a reflector, before the target, just a little to one side. It
lighted up the target beautifully; and I believe there was a better chance of hitting it
than by daylight, for the only thing you
could see was the target, and so your atten-

tion was not distracted. To be sure," he said, in answer to a question, "it was a good deal of trouble to find the arrows, but that I always have. When I get so expert that I can put all the arrows into the target, there will be no trouble of the kind, night or day. However," he continued, "I don't practise any more by night. The other evening I sent an arrow slam-bang into the lantern, and broke it all to flinders. Borrowed lantern, too. Besides, I found it made Miss Martha very nervous to have me shooting about the house after dark. She had a friend, who had a little boy, who was hit in the leg by an arrow from a bow, which, she says, accidentally went off in the night, of its own accord. She is certainly a little mixed in her mind in regard to this matter; but I wished to respect her feelings, and so shall not use another lantern."

As I have said, there were many good archers among the ladies of our club. Some of them, after we had been organised for a month or two, made scores that few of the gentlemen could excel. But the lady who attracted the greatest attention when she shot was Miss Rosa.

When this very pretty young lady stood up before the ladies' target—her left side well advanced, her bow firmly held out in her strong left arm, which never quivered, her head a little bent to the right, her arrow drawn back by three well-gloved fingers to the tip of her little ear, her dark eyes steadily fixed upon the gold, and her dress — well fitted over her fine and vigorous figure— falling in graceful folds about her feet, we all stopped shooting to look at her.

" There is something statuesque about her," said Pepton, who ardently admired her, "and yet there isn't. A statue could never equal her unless we knew there was a probability of movement in it. And the only statues which have that are the Jarley wax-works, which she does not resemble in the least. There is only one thing that that girl needs to make her a perfect archer, and that is to be able to aim better."

This was true. Miss Rosa did need to aim better. Her arrows had a curious habit of going on all sides of the target, and it was very seldom that one chanced to stick into it. For, if she did make a hit, we all knew it was chance, and that there was no probability of her doing it again. Once she put an arrow right into the centre of the gold,—one of the finest shots ever made on the ground,—but she didn't hit the target

again for two weeks. She was almost as bad
a shot as Pepton, and that is saying a good
deal.

One evening I was sitting with Pepton
on the little front porch of the old ladies'
house where we were taking our after-dinner
smoke while Miss Martha and Miss Maria
were washing, with their own white hands,
the china and glass in which they took so
much pride. I often used to come over and
spend an hour with Pepton. He liked to
have some one to whom he could talk on the
subjects which filled his soul, and I liked to
hear him talk.

"I tell you," said he, as he leaned back
in his chair, with his feet carefully disposed
on the railing so that they would not injure
Miss Maria's Madeira vine, "I tell you, sir,
that there are two things I crave with all
my power of craving ; two goals I fain would
reach ; two diadems I would wear upon my
brow. One of these is to kill an eagle—or
some large bird—with a shaft from my good
bow. I would then have it stuffed and
mounted, with the very arrow that killed
it still sticking in its breast. This trophy
of my skill I would have fastened against
the wall of my room, or my hall, and I
would feel proud to think that my grand-

B. M. L

children could point to that bird—which I
would carefully bequeath to my descendants
—and say, 'My grand'ther shot that bird,
and with that very arrow.' Would it not
stir your pulses, if you could do a thing like
that?"

"I should have to stir them up a good
deal before I could do it," I replied. "It
would be a hard thing to shoot an eagle with
an arrow. If you want a stuffed bird to
bequeath, you'd better use a rifle."

"A rifle!" exclaimed Pepton. "There
would be no glory in that. There are lots
of birds shot with rifles,—eagles, hawks,
wild geese, tom-tits——"

"Oh no!" I interrupted, "not tom-tits."

"Well, perhaps they are too little for
a rifle," said he; "but what I mean to say
is, that I wouldn't care at all for an eagle I
had shot with a rifle. You couldn't show
the ball that killed him. If it were put
in properly, it would be inside, where it
couldn't be seen. No, sir; it is ever so
much more honourable, and far more difficult, too, to hit an eagle than to hit a target."

"That is very true," I answered, "especially in these days, when there are so few
eagles and so many targets. But what is
your other diadem?"

"That," said Pepton, "is to see Miss Rosa wear the badge."

"Indeed!" said I ; and from that moment I began to understand Pepton's hopes in regard to the grandmother of those children who should point to the eagle.

"Yes, sir," he continued, "I should be truly happy to see her win the badge. And she ought to win it. No one shoots more correctly, and with a better understanding of all the rules, than she does. There must, truly, be something the matter with her aiming. I've half a mind to coach her a little."

I turned aside to see who was coming down the road. I would not have had him know I smiled.

The most objectionable person in our club was O. J. Hollingsworth. He was a good enough fellow in himself, but it was as an archer that we objected to him. There was, so far as I know, scarcely a rule of archery that he did not habitually violate. Our president and nearly all of us remonstrated with him, and Pepton even went to see him on the subject ; but it was all to no purpose. With a quiet disregard of other people's ideas about bow-shooting and other people's opinions about himself, he persevered in a style of shooting which appeared absolutely absurd to any one who knew anything of the rules and methods of archery.

I used to like to look at him when his turn came around to shoot. He was not such a pleasing object of vision as Miss Rosa, but his style was so entirely novel to me that it was interesting. He held the bow horizontally, instead of perpendicularly, like other archers; and he held it well down —about opposite his waistband. He did not draw his arrow back to his ear, but he drew it back to the lower button of his vest. Instead of standing upright, with his left side to the target, he faced it full, and leaned forward over his arrow, in an attitude which reminded me of a Roman soldier about to fall upon his sword. When he had seized the nock of his arrow between his finger and thumb, he languidly glanced at the target, raised his bow a little, and let fly. The provoking thing about it was that he nearly always hit. If he had only known how to stand, and hold his bow, and draw back his arrow, he would have been a very good archer. But, as it was, we could not help laughing at him, although our president always discountenanced anything of the kind.

Our Champion was a tall man, very cool and steady, who went to work at archery exactly as if he were paid a salary, and intended to earn his money honestly. He did the best he could in every way. He generally shot with one of the bows owned by the club; but if any one on the ground had a better one, he would borrow it. He used to shoot sometimes with Pepton's bow, which he declared to be a most capital one; but as Pepton was always very nervous when he saw his bow in the hands of another than himself, the Champion soon ceased to borrow it.

There were two badges, one of green silk and gold, for the ladies, and one of green and red, for the gentlemen; and these were shot for at each weekly meeting. With the exception of a few times, when the club was first formed, the Champion had always worn the gentlemen's badge. Many of us tried hard to win it from him; but we never could succeed—he shot too well.

On the morning of one of our meeting days, the Champion told me, as I was going to the city with him, that he should not be able to return at his usual hour that afternoon. He would be very busy, and should have to wait for the 6.15 train, which would bring him home too late for the archery meeting. So he gave me the badge, asking me to hand it to the president, that he might bestow it on the successful competitor that afternoon.

We were all rather glad that the Champion was obliged to be absent. Here was a chance for some one of us to win the badge. It was not, indeed, an opportunity for us to win a great deal of honour, for if the Champion were to be there, we should have no chance at all ; but we were satisfied with this much, having no reason—in the present, at least—to expect anything more.

So we went to the targets with a new zeal, and most of us shot better than we had ever shot before. In this number was O. J. Hollingsworth. He excelled himself, and, what was worse, he excelled all the rest of us. He actually made a score of eighty-five in twenty-four shots, which at that time was remarkably good shooting, for our club. This was dreadful ! To have a fellow, who didn't know how to shoot, beat us all, was too bad. If any visitor who knew anything at all of archery should see that the member who wore the champion's badge was a man who held his bow as if he had the stomach-ache, it would ruin

our character as a club. It was not to be
borne.

Pepton, in particular, felt greatly out-
raged. We had met very promptly that
afternoon, and had finished our regular
shooting much earlier than usual ; and now
a knot of us were gathered together, talking
over this unfortunate occurrence.

"I don't intend to stand it," Pepton suddenly exclaimed. "I feel it as a personal
disgrace. I'm going to have the Champion
here before dark. By the rules, he has a
right to shoot until the president declares it
is too late. Some of you fellows stay here,
and I'll bring him."

And away he ran, first giving me charge
of his precious bow. There was no need of
his asking us to stay. We were bound to
see the fun out ; and to fill up the time our
president offered a special prize of a handsome bouquet from his gardens, to be shot
for by the ladies.

Pepton ran to the railroad station, and
telegraphed to the Champion. This was his
message—

"You are absolutely needed here. If possible,
take the 5.30 train for Ackford. I will drive
over for you. Answer."

There was no train before the 6.15 by which the Champion could come directly to our village; but Ackford, a small town about three miles distant, was on another railroad, on which there were frequent after-noon trains.

The Champion answered—

"All right.   Meet me."

Then Pepton rushed to our livery stable, hired a horse and buggy, and drove to Ack-ford.

A little after half-past six, when several of us were beginning to think that Pepton had failed in his plans, he drove rapidly into the grounds, making a very short turn at the gate, and pulled up his panting horse just in time to avoid running over three ladies, who were seated on the grass.   The Champion was by his side !

The latter lost no time in talking or saluations.   He knew what he had been brought there to do, and he immediately set about trying to do it.   He took Pepton's bow, which the latter urged upon him; he stood up, straight and firm on the line, at thirty-five yards from the gentlemen's target; he carefully selected his arrows, examining the feathers and wiping away any bit of soil that might be adhering to the points after some one had shot them into the turf; with vigorous arm he drew each arrow to its head; he fixed his eyes and his whole mind on the centre of the target; he shot his twenty-four arrows, handed to him, one by one, by Pepton, and he made a score of ninety-one.

The whole club had been scoring the shots as they were made, and when the last arrow plumped into the red ring, a cheer arose from every member excepting three: the Champion, the president, and O. J. Hollingsworth. But Pepton cheered loudly enough to make up these deficiencies.

"What in the mischief did they cheer him for?" asked Hollingsworth of me. "They didn't cheer me, when I beat everybody on the grounds, an hour ago. And it's no new thing for him to win the badge; he does it every time."

"Well," said I frankly, "I think the club, *as* a club, objects to your wearing the badge, because you don't know how to shoot."

"Don't know how to shoot!" he cried. "Why, I can hit the target better than any of you. Isn't that what you try to do when you shoot?"

"Yes," said I, "of course that is what we try to do. But we try to do it in the proper way."

"Proper grandmother!" he exclaimed. "It don't seem to help you much. The best thing you fellows can do is to learn to shoot my way, and then perhaps you may be able to hit oftener."

When the Champion had finished shooting, he went home to his dinner, but many of us stood about, talking over our great escape.

"I feel as if I had done that myself," said Pepton. "I am almost as proud as if I had shot—well, not an eagle, but a soaring lark."

"Why, that ought to make you prouder than the other," said I; "for a lark, especially when it's soaring, must be a good deal harder to hit than an eagle."

"That's so," said Pepton reflectively; "but I'll stick to the lark. I'm proud."

During the next month our style of archery improved very much, so much, indeed, that we increased our distance, for gentlemen, to forty yards, and that for ladies to thirty, and also had serious thoughts of challenging the Ackford club to a match. But as this was generally understood to be a crack club, we finally determined to defer our challenge until the next season.

When I say we improved, I do not mean all of us. I do not mean Miss Rosa. Although her attitudes were as fine as ever, and every motion as true to rule as ever, she seldom made a hit. Pepton actually did try to teach her how to aim; but the various methods of pointing the arrow which he suggested resulted in such wild shooting, that the boys who picked up the arrows never dared to stick the points of their noses beyond their boarded barricade during Miss Rosa's turns at the target. But she was not discouraged; and Pepton often assured her that if she would keep up a good heart, and practise regularly, she would get the badge yet. As a rule, Pepton was so honest and truthful that a little statement of this kind, especially under the circumstances, might be forgiven him.

One day Pepton came to me and announced that he had made a discovery.

"It's about archery," he said; "and I don't mind telling you, because I know you will not go about telling everybody else, and also because I want to see you succeed as an archer."

"I am very much obliged," I said; "and what is the discovery?"

"It's this," he answered. "When you draw your bow, bring the nock of your arrow"—he was always very particular about technical terms—"well up to your ear. Having done that, don't bother any more about your right hand. It has nothing to do with the correct pointing of your arrow, for it must be kept close to your right ear, just as if it were screwed there. Then with your left hand bring around the bow so that your fist—with the arrow-head, which is resting on top of it—shall point, as nearly as you can make it, directly at the centre of the target. Then let fly, and ten to one you'll make a hit. Now, what do you think of that, for a discovery? I've thoroughly tested the plan, and it works splendidly."

"I think," said I, "that you have discovered the way in which good archers shoot. You have stated the correct method of managing a bow and arrow."

"Then you don't think it's an original method with me?"

"Certainly not," I answered.

"But it's the correct way?"

"There's no doubt of that," said I.

"Well," said Pepton, "then I shall make it my way."

He did so; and the consequence was that one day, when the Champion happened to be away, Pepton won the badge. When the result was announced, we were all surprised, but none so much so as Pepton himself. He had been steadily improving since he had adopted a good style of shooting, but he had had no idea that he would that day be able to win the badge.

When our president pinned the emblem of success upon the lapel of his coat, Pepton turned pale, and then he flushed. He thanked the president, and was about to thank the ladies and gentlemen; but probably recollecting that we had had nothing to do with it,—unless, indeed, we had shot badly on his behalf,—he refrained. He said little, but I could see that he was very proud and very happy. There was but one drawback to his triumph: Miss Rosa was not there. She was a very regular attendant, but for some reason she was absent on this momentous afternoon. I did not say anything to him on the subject, but I knew he felt this absence deeply.

But this cloud could not wholly overshadow his happiness. He walked home alone, his face beaming, his eyes sparkling, and his good bow under his arm.

That evening I called on him; for I thought that, when he had cooled down a little, he would like to talk over the affair. But he was not in. Miss Maria said that he had gone out as soon as he had finished his dinner, which he hurried through in a way which would certainly injure his digestion if he kept up the practice; and dinner was late, too, for they waited for him; and the archery meeting lasted a long time to-day; and it really was not right for him to stay out after the dew began to fall with only ordinary shoes on, for what's the good of knowing how to shoot a bow and arrow, if you're laid up in your bed with rheumatism or disease of the lungs! Good old lady! She would have kept Pepton in a green baize bag, had such a thing been possible.

The next morning, full two hours before church-time, Pepton called on me. His face was still beaming. I could not help smiling.

"Your happiness lasts well," I said.

"Lasts!" he exclaimed. "Why shouldn't it last!"

"There's no reason why it should not—at

least for a week," I said. "And even longer, if you repeat your success."

I did not feel so much like congratulating Pepton as I had on the previous evening. I thought he was making too much of his badge-winning.

"Look here !" said Pepton, seating himself, and drawing his chair close to me, "you are shooting wild—very wild indeed. You don't even see the target. Let me tell you something. Last evening I went to see Miss Rosa. She was delighted at my success. I had not expected this. I thought she would be pleased, but not to such a degree. Her congratulations were so warm that they set me on fire."

"They must have been very warm indeed," I remarked.

" 'Miss Rosa,' said I," continued Pepton, without regarding my interruption, " 'it has been my fondest hope to see you wear the badge.' 'But I never could get it, you know,' she said. 'You have got it,' I exclaimed. 'Take this. I won it for you. Make me happy by wearing it.' 'I can't do that,' she said. 'That is a gentleman's badge.' 'Take it,' I cried, 'gentleman and all !'

" I can't tell you all that happened after that," continued Pepton. " You know it wouldn't do. It is enough to say that she wears the badge. And we are both her own —the badge and I!"

Now I congratulated him in good earnest. There was a reason for it.

"I don't care a snap now for shooting an eagle," said Pepton, springing to his feet, and striding up and down the floor. "Let 'em all fly free for me. I have made the most glorious shot that man could make. I have hit the gold — hit it fair in the very centre! And what's more, I've knocked it clean out of the target! Nobody else can ever make such a shot. The rest of you fellows will have to be content to hit the red, the blue, the black, or the white. The gold is mine!"

I called on the old ladies, some time after this, and found them alone. They were generally alone in the evenings now. We talked about Pepton's engagement, and I found them resigned. They were sorry to lose him, but they wanted him to be happy.

"We have always known," said Miss Martha, with a little sigh, "that we must die, and that he must get married. But we don't intend to repine. These things will come to people." And her little sigh was followed by a smile, still smaller.

A STORY OF ASSISTED FATE.

A STORY OF ASSISTED FATE

I.

IN a general way I am not a superstitious man, but I have a few ideas, or notions, in regard to fatality and kindred subjects of which I have never been able entirely to dispossess my mind ; nor can I say that I have ever tried very much to do so, for I hold that a certain amount of irrationalism in the nature of a man is a thing to be desired. By its aid he clambers over the wall which limits the action of his intellect, and if he be but sure that he can get back again no harm may come of it, while he is the better for many pleasant excursions.

My principal superstitious notion, and indeed the only one of importance, is the belief that whatever I earnestly desire and plan for will happen. This idea does not relate to things for which people fight hard, or work long, but to those events for which we sit down and wait. It is truly a pleasant

belief, and one worthy to be fostered if there
can be found any ground for it. I do not
exercise my little superstition very often,
but when I do I find things happen as I
wish; and in cases where this has not yet
occurred there is plenty of time to wait.

I am not a very old person, being now in
my twenty-eighth year, but my two sisters,
who live with me, as well as most of my ac-
quaintances, look upon me, I think, as an
older man. This is not due to my experience in the world, for I have not gone out a
great deal among my fellow-men, but rather
to my habits of reading and reflection, which
have so matured my intellectual nature that
the rest of me, so to speak, has insensibly
stepped a little faster to keep pace with it.
Grace Anna, indeed, is two years older than
I, yet I know she looks up to me as a senior
quite as much as does Bertha, who is but
twenty-four.

These sisters had often laughingly assured
me that the one thing I needed was a wife,
and, although I never spoke much on the
subject, in the course of time I began to
think a good deal about it, and the matter
so interested my mind that at last I did a
very singular thing. I keep a diary, in which
I briefly note daily events, especially those

which may, in a degree, be considered as epochs. My book has a page for every day, with the date printed at the top thereof ; not a very desirable form, perhaps, for those who would write much on one day and very little the next, but it suits me well enough, for I seldom enter into details. Not many months ago, as I sat alone, one evening, in my library, turning over the leaves of this diary, I looked ahead at the pages intended for the days of the year that were yet to come, and the thought entered my mind that it was a slavish thing to be able to note only what had happened, and not to dare to write one word upon the blank pages of the next month, or the next, or even of to-morrow. As I turned backward and forward these pages devoted to a record of the future the desire came to me to write something upon one of them. It was a foolish fancy, perhaps, but it pleased me. I would like a diary, not only of what had been, but of what was to be. I longed to challenge fate, and I did it. I selected a page, not too far ahead and in a good time of the year,—it was September 14th,—and on it I wrote—

"This day came into my life she who is to be my wife."

When I had made this strange entry I regarded it with satisfaction. I had fully come to the conclusion that it was due to my position as the owner of a goodly estate that I should marry. I had felt that at some time I must do something in this matter. And now a thing was done, and a time was fixed. It is true that I knew no woman who was at all likely, upon the day I had selected, or upon any other day, to exercise a matrimonial influence upon my life. But that made no difference to me. I had taken my fate into my own hands, and I would now see what would happen.

It was then early in July, and in a little more than two months the day which I had made a very momentous one to me would arrive. I cannot say that I had a positive belief that what I had written would occur on the 14th of September, but I had a very strange notion that, as there was no reason why it should not be so, it would be so. At any rate, who could say it would not be so? This sort of thing was not a belief, but to all intents and purposes it was just as good.

It was somewhat amusing even to myself, and it would probably have been very amusing to any one else acquainted with the cir-

cumstances, to observe the influence that
this foundationless and utterly irrational
expectation had upon me.   To the great
delight of my sisters, I began to attend
to matters in which formerly I had taken
little interest.   I set two men at work upon
the grounds about the house, giving my
personal supervision to the removal of the
patches of grass in the driveway, which led
under the oaks to the door.   Here and there
I had a panel of fence put in better order,
and a dead apple-tree, which for some time
had stood on the brow of a hill in view of
the house, was cut down and taken away.

"If any of our friends think of visiting
us," said Bertha, "they ought to come now,
while everything is looking so trim and
nice."

"Would you like that?" asked Grace
Anna, looking at me.

"Yes," I replied.   "That is, they might
begin to come now."

At this both my sisters laughed.

"Begin to come!" cried Bertha.   "How
hospitable you are growing!"

The summer went on, and I kept good
faith with my little superstition.   If either
of us should desert the other, it should not
be I who would do it.   It pleased me to look

forward to the event which I had called
up out of the future, and to wait for it—if
perchance it should come.

One morning my sister Bertha entered my
library, with a letter in her hand and a very
pleasant expression on her face. "What do
you think?" she said. "We are going to
have a visit!—just as the paint is dry on the
back porch, so that we can have tea there in
the afternoon."

"A visit!" I exclaimed, regarding her
with much interest.

"Yes," continued Bertha. "Kitty Watridge is coming to stay with us. I have
written and written to her, and now she is
coming."

"Who is she?" I asked.

Bertha laughed. "You haven't forgotten
the Watridges, have you?"

No, I had not forgotten them; at least,
the only one of them I ever knew. Old Mr.
Watridge had been a friend of my late
father, a cheerful and rather ruddy man,
although much given to books. He had
been my friend, too, in the days when he
used to come to us; and I remember well
that it was he who started me on a journey
along the third shelf from the top, on the
east wall of the library, through "The World

Displayed," in many volumes, by Smart, Goldsmith, and Johnson; and thence to some "New Observations on Italy," in French, by two Swedish gentlemen, in 1758; and so on through many other works of the kind, where I found the countries shown forth on their quaint pages so different from those of the same name described in modern books of travel that it was to me a virtual enlargement of the world. It had been a long time since I had seen the old gentleman, and I felt sorry for it.

"Is Mr. Watridge coming?" I asked.

"Of course not," said Bertha. "That would be your affair. And besides, he never leaves home now. It is only Kitty, his youngest daughter, my friend."

I had an indistinct recollection that Mr. Watridge had some children, and that they were daughters, but that was all I remembered about them. "She is grown?" I asked.

"I should think so," answered Bertha, with a laugh. "She is at least twenty."

If my sister could have known the intense interest which suddenly sprung up within me she would have been astounded. A grown-up, marriageable young lady was coming to my house, in September! My next question was asked hurriedly : " When will she be here ? "

"She is coming next Wednesday, the 16th," answered Bertha, referring to her letter.

"The 16th !" I said to myself. "That is two days after my date."

" What kind of a lady is she?" I asked Bertha.

"She is lovely,—just as lovely as she can be."

I now began to feel a little disappointed. If she were lovely, as my sister said, and twenty, with good Watridge blood, why did she not come a little sooner? It was truly an odd thing to do, but I could not forbear expressing what I thought. "I wish," I said, somewhat abstractedly, "that she were coming on Monday instead of Wednesday."

Bertha laughed heartily. "I was really afraid," she said, "that you might think there were enough girls already in the house. But here you are wanting Kitty to come before she is ready. Grace Anna !" she cried to my elder sister, who was passing the open door, "he isn't put out a bit, and he is in such a hurry to see Kitty that he thinks she should come on Monday."

It was impossible to chide my sisters for laughing at me, and I could not help smiling myself. "It is not that I am in a hurry to see her," I observed, "for I do not know the young lady at all ; but I consider Monday a more suitable day than Wednesday for her arrival."

"It is odd," replied Bertha, "that you should prefer one day to another."

"Is there any reason why it does not suit you to have her come on Wednesday ?" asked Grace Anna. "Her visit might be deferred a day or two."

Of course I could give no reason, and I did not wish the visit deferred.

"It's just because he's so dreadfully systematic !" cried Bertha. "He thinks everything ought to begin at the beginning of the week, and that even a visit should make a fair start on Monday, and not break in unmethodically."

My elder sister was always very considerate of my welfare and my wishes, and had it been practicable I believe that she would have endeavoured in this instance to make our hospitality conform to what appeared to be my love of system and order. But she explained to me that, apart from the awkwardness of asking the young lady

to change the day which she had herself fixed,
without being able to give any good reason
therefor, it would be extremely inconvenient
for them to have their visitor before Wednesday, as an earlier arrival would materially interfere with certain household arrangements.

I said no more, but I was disappointed ;
and this feeling grew upon me, for the reason
that during the rest of the day and the evening my sisters talked a great deal about their
young friend, and I found that, unless they
were indeed most prejudiced judges,—which
in the case of Grace Anna, at least, I could
never believe,—this young person who was
coming to us must be possessed of most admirable personal qualities. She was pretty ;
she had excellent moral sentiments, a well-
cultured intellect, and a lovable disposition.
These, with the good blood,—which, in my
opinion, was a most important requisite,—
made up a woman in every way fitted to
enter my life in a matrimonial capacity. If,
without any personal bias, I had been select-
ing a wife for a friend, I could not have expected to do better than this. That such a
young person should come within the range
of my cognisance on the wrong day would
be, to say the least, a most annoying occurrence. Why did I not select the 16th, or

she the 14th? A fate that was two days
slow might as well be no fate at all. My
meeting with the girl would have no meaning. I must admit that the more I thought
about this girl the more I wished it should
have a meaning.

During the night, or perhaps very early
in the morning, a most felicitous idea came
into my mind. I would assist my fate. My
idea was this: On Monday I would drive to
Mr. Watridge's house. It was a pleasant
day's journey. I would spend Tuesday with
him, and, returning on Wednesday, I could
bring Miss Kitty with me. Thus all the
necessary conditions would be fulfilled. She
would come into my life on the 14th, and I
would have opportunities of knowing her
which probably would not occur to me at
home. Everything would happen as it
should; only, instead of the lady coming
to me, I should go to her.

As I expected, my project, when I announced it at the breakfast table, was the
occasion of much mirth, especially on the
part of Bertha. "I never saw anything
like it!" she cried. "You want to see
Kitty even more than I do. I should never
have thought of such a thing as going for
her two days in advance."

"As it would have been impossible for you to do so," said I, "I can easily conceive that you would not have allowed the idea to enter your mind."

Grace Anna, however, looked upon my plan with much favour, and entered into its details with interest, dwelling particularly on the pleasure Mr. Watridge would derive from my visit.

I looked forward with great pleasure to the little journey I was about to make. The distance from Eastover, my residence, to Mr. Watridge's house was some twenty-five miles,—a very suitable day's drive in fine weather. The road led through a pleasant country, with several opportunities for pretty views; and about half-way was a neat tavern, standing behind an immense cherry-tree, where a stop could be made for rest and for a midday meal. I had a comfortable, easy-cushioned buggy, well provided with protective appurtenances in case of rain or too much sunshine; and my sisters and myself were of the opinion that, under ordinary circumstances, no one would hesitate between this vehicle and the crowded stage-coach, which was the only means of communication between our part of the country and that in which the Watridge estate lay.

I made an early start on Monday morning, with my good horse, Dom Pedro; named by my sister Bertha, but whether for the Emperor of Brazil, or for a social game of cards which we generally played when we had two or three visitors, and therefore there were too many of us for whist, I do not know.   I arrived at my destination towards the close of the afternoon, and old Mr. Watridge was delighted to see me.   We spent a pleasant hour in his library, waiting for the return of his two daughters, who were out for a walk.   It must be admitted that it was with considerable emotional perturbation that I beheld the entrance into that room of Miss Kitty Watridge.   She came in alone; her sister, who was much older, being detained by some household duties, connected, probably, with my unexpected arrival.   This,. with the action of Mr. Watridge in presently excusing himself for a time, gave me an opportunity, more immediate than I had expected, for an uninterrupted study of this young lady, who had become to me so important a person.

I will not describe Kitty, her appearance, nor her conversation, but will merely remark that before we were joined by her father and sister I would have been quite willing, so far as I was concerned, to show her the entry in my diary.

It may be that a man heavily clad with the armour of reserve and restraint sinks more quickly and deeper than one not so encumbered, when he finds himself suddenly in a current of that sentiment which now possessed me. Be that as it may, my determination was arrived at before I slept that night: Kitty Watridge had entered into my life on the 14th of September, and I was willing to accept her as my wife.

As the son of an old comrade on the part of the father, and as the brother of two dear friends on the part of the daughters, I was treated with hearty cordiality by his family, and the next day was a most pleasing and even delightful one to me, until the evening came. Then a cloud, and a very heavy one, arose upon my emotional horizon. I had stated how I purposed to make the little journey of Miss Kitty to our house more comfortable and expeditious than it would otherwise be, and Mr. Watridge had expressed himself very much pleased with the plan ; while Kitty had declared that it would be charming, especially when compared with travel by stage-coach, of which the principal features, in her idea of it, appeared to be mothers, little children, and lunch baskets. But, after dinner, Miss Maria, the elder daughter, remarked very quietly, but very positively, that she did not think it would do—that is the phrase she used—for me to drive her sister to East-over. She gave no reasons, and I asked none, but it was quite evident that her decision was not one to be altered.

"It would be far better," she said, "not to change our original plan, and for Kitty, as well as her trunk, to go by the stage. Mrs. Karcroft is going the whole of the way, and Kitty will be well taken care of."

Miss Maria was the head of the house; she had acted for many years as the maternal director of her sister; and I saw very soon that what the other two members of the family might think upon the subject would matter very little. The father, indeed, made at first some very vigorous dissent, urging that it would be a shame to make me take that long drive home alone, when I had ex-pected company; and although Kitty said nothing, I am sure she looked quite dis-appointed. But neither words nor looks availed anything. Miss Maria was placid,

but very firm, and under her deft manage-
ment of the conversation the subject was
soon dismissed as settled.

"I am very sorry," observed the old gentleman to me, when the ladies had bidden
us good-night, "that Kitty cannot take advantage of your invitation, which was a very
kind one, and to which I see not the slightest objection.   My daughter Maria has very
peculiar ideas sometimes, but as she acts as
a sort of mother here we don't like to interfere with her."

"I would not have you do so for the
world," answered I.

"You are very good, very good!" exclaimed Mr. Watridge; "and I must say I
think it's a confounded shame that you and
Kitty cannot take that pleasant drive together.   Suppose you go with her in the
stage, and let me send a man to Eastover
with your horse and vehicle."

"I thank you very kindly, sir," I replied,
"but it will be better for me to return the
way I came; and your daughter will have a
companion, I understand."

"Nobody but old Mrs. Karcroft, and she
counts for nothing as company.   You had
better think of it."

I would not consent, however, to make

any change in my arrangements; and, shortly after, I retired.

I went to bed that night a very angry man. When I prepared a plan or scheme with which no reasonable fault could be found, I was not accustomed to have it thwarted, or indeed even objected to. I was displeased with Mr. Watridge because he allowed himself to be so easily influenced, and I was even dissatisfied with Kitty's want of spirit, though of course she could not have been expected to exhibit an eagerness to accompany me. But with that horrible old maid, Miss Maria, I was truly indignant. There frequently arises in the mind an image which forcibly connects itself with the good or bad qualities of a person under our contemplation, and thus Miss Maria appeared to me in the character of a moral pepper-box. Virtue is like sugar or cream,—good in itself, and of advantage to that with which it is suitably mingled; but Miss Maria's propriety was the hottest and most violent sort of pepper, extremely disagreeable in itself, and never needed except in the case of weak moral digestion. Her objections were an insult to me. I went to sleep thinking of a little pepper cruet which I would like to have made of silver for my table, to take the place of the owl or other conventional pattern, which should be exactly like Miss Maria,—hard and unimpressionable without, hollow within, and the top of its head perforated with little holes. At breakfast I endeavoured to be coldly polite, but it must have been easy for the family to perceive that I was very much offended.   I requested that my horse and buggy should be made ready as soon as possible.   While I was waiting for it on the porch, where Mr. Watridge had just left me, Miss Kitty came out to me.   This was the first time I had been alone with her since the preceding afternoon, when we had had a most charming walk through the orchard and over the hills to a high point, where we had stayed until we saw the sun go down.

"It seems a real pity," she observed very prettily, and in a tone which touched me, "that you should be driving off now by yourself, while in about an hour I shall start from the same place."

"Miss Kitty," said I, "would you like to go with me?"

She hesitated for a moment, looked down, and then looked up, and said, "So far as I am concerned, I think—I mean I know—

that I should like very much to go with you. But you see "—and then she hesitated again.

"Say no more, I pray you!" I exclaimed. I would not place her in the unpleasant position of defending, or even explaining, the unwarrantable interference of a relative. "If you really wish to accompany me," I continued, warmly shaking her hand, for my buggy was now approaching, "I am entirely satisfied, and nothing more need be said. It is, in a measure, the same as if you were going with me. Good-bye."

A moment before I was depressed and morose. Now I was exuberantly joyful. The change was sudden, but there was reason for it. Kitty wished to go with me, and had come to tell me so!

Mr. Watridge and his elder daughter now appeared in the doorway, and as I took leave of the latter I am sure she noticed a change in my manner. I said no more to her than was absolutely necessary, but the sudden cheerfulness which had taken possession of me could not be repressed even in her presence.

The old gentleman accompanied me to the carriage-block. "I don't want to bore you about it," he said, "but I really am sorry you are going away alone."

I felt quite sure, from several things Mr. Watridge had said and done during my visit, that he would be well pleased to see his younger daughter and myself thrown very much into the company of each other, and to have us remain so, indeed, for the rest of our lives. And there was no reason why he should not desire it. In every way the conditions of such a union would be most favourable.

"Thank you very much," I returned; "but the pleasure of having your daughter at my house will make me forget this little disappointment."

He looked at me with glistening eyes. Had I boldly asked him, "Will you be my father-in-law?" no more favourable answer could have come from his lips than I now saw upon his countenance.

"Good fortune be with you!" were his last words as I drove away.

I do not suppose anything of the kind could be more delightful than my drive that morning. Miss Kitty had said that she would like to be my companion, and I determined to have her so in imagination, if not in fact. The pleasures of fancy are sometimes more satisfactory than those of reality, for we have them entirely under our control. I chose now to imagine that Miss Kitty was seated by my side, and I sat well to the right, that I might give her plenty of room. In imagination I conversed with her, and she answered me as I would have her. Our remarks were carefully graduated to the duration of our acquaintance and the seemly progress of our intimacy. I wished to discover the intellectual status of the fair young creature who had come into my life on the 14th of September. I spoke to her of books, and found that her reading had been varied and judicious. She had read Farrar's *Life of Christ*, but did not altogether like it; and while she had much enjoyed Froude's *Cæsar*, she could have wished to believe the author as just as he endeavoured to make his hero appear. With modern romance she had dealt but lightly, rather preferring works of history and travel, even when pervaded with the flavour of the eighteenth century. But we did not always speak of abstract subjects ; we were both susceptible to the influences of nature, and my companion enjoyed as much as I did the bright sunshine tempered by a cooling breeze, the clear sky with fair white clouds floating along the horizon, and the occasional views of the blue and distant mountains,

their tops suffused with warm autumnal
mists.   After a time I asked her if I might
call her Kitty, and glancing downward, and
then up, with the same look she had given
me on the porch, she said I might.   This
was very pleasant, and was not, in my
opinion, an undue familiarity, which fea-
ture I was very careful to eliminate from
our companionship.   One act, however, of
what might be termed super-friendly kindness I intended to propose, and the contemplation of its   probable   acceptance
afforded me much pleasure.   After our
quiet luncheon in the shaded little dining-
room of the Cherry-Tree Inn, and when she
had rested as long as she chose, we would
begin our afternoon journey, and the road,
before very long, would lead us through a
great pine wood.   Here, rolling over the
hard, smooth way, and breathing the gentle
odour of the pines, she would naturally feel
a little somnolent, and I intended to say to
her that if she liked she might rest her head
upon my shoulder, and doze.   If I should
hear the sound of approaching wheels I
would gently arouse her; but as an interruption of this kind was not likely to occur,
I thought with much satisfaction of the pleasure I should have in the afternoon, when

this fancy would be appropriate. To look upon the little head gently resting on that shoulder, which, when our acquaintance had more fully developed, I would offer her as a permanent possession, would be to me a preconnubial satisfaction of a very high order.

When about a mile from the Cherry-Tree Inn, and with my mind filled with these agreeable fancies, an accident happened to me. One of the irons which connected the shafts to the front axle broke, and the conditions of my progress became abruptly changed. The wheel at that end of the axle to which a shaft was yet attached went suddenly forward, and the other flew back and grated against the side of the buggy, while both wheels, instead of rolling in the general course of the vehicle, were dragged in a sidewise direction. The disconnected shaft fell upon the legs of Dom Pedro, who, startled by the unusual sensation, forsook his steady trot, and broke into a run. Thus, with the front wheels scraping the road, the horse attached but by a single shaft, I was hurried along at an alarming pace. Pull as I might, I could not check the progress of Dom Pedro; and if this state of affairs had continued for

more than the few moments which it really
lasted, the front wheels would have been
shattered, and I do not know what sad
results might have ensued.   But the other
shaft broke loose, the reins were rudely torn
from my hands, and the horse, now free
from attachment to the vehicle, went clat-
tering along the road, the shafts bobbing at
his heels; while the buggy, following the
guidance of the twisted front axle, ran into
a shallow ditch at the side of the road, and
abruptly stopped.

Unhurt I sprang out, and my first thought
was one of joy that the Kitty who had been
by my side was an imaginary one.   Had the
real Kitty been there, what might not have
happened to her !   A dozen possible acci-
dents crowded themselves on my mind, and
I have no doubt my countenance expressed
my feelings.

There was nothing to be done but to take
my valise and the whip from the buggy, and
walk on to the inn, where I found the landlord in the act of saddling a horse, to come
and see what had happened to me.   Dom
Pedro had arrived with a portion of the
shafts attached to him, the rest having been
kicked away.   The accident occasioned considerable stir at the inn; but as I never

cared to discuss my personal affairs any further than is necessary, it was soon arranged that after I had lunched I would borrow a saddle from the landlord, and ride Dom Pedro home, while the broken buggy would be brought to the inn, where I would send for it the next day.   This plan did not please me, for I was not fond of equestrianism, and Dom Pedro was rather a hard trotter; but there was nothing better to do. Had I not taken this road, which was much more agreeable although rather longer than the high road, I might have been picked up by the stage which was conveying Miss Kitty to my house.

While I was yet at my meal there arrived at the inn a young man, who shortly afterward entered the room, and informed me that, having heard of my accident, he came to offer me a seat in the buggy in which he was travelling.   He was going my way, and would be glad of a companion.   This invitation, given as it was by a well-appearing young man of pleasing manners, was, after a little consideration, accepted by me.   I would much prefer to ride a dozen miles in a buggy with a stranger than on horseback alone.

The drive of the afternoon was very different from what I had expected it to be, but it was not devoid of some pleasant features. My companion was sociable, and not too communicative; although he annoyed me very much by giving me the entirely un-called-for information that if I had had short straps from the ends of the shafts to the axle, which no well-ordered buggy should be without, the accident would not have occurred. I passed this by, and our conversation became more general, and to me more acceptable. The young man was going to Harnden, a village not far from my house, where he appeared to have some business, and he assured me that he would not object in the least to go a little out of his way and set me down at my door.

We reached Eastover quite late in the afternoon, and I perceived, from the group on the porch, that Miss Kitty had arrived. All three of the ladies came down to meet me, evidently very much surprised to see me in a strange vehicle. When I alighted, and was hastily explaining to my sisters the cause of this change of conveyance, I was surprised to see Miss Kitty shaking hands with the young man, who was standing by his horse's head. My elder sister, Grace Anna, who had also noticed this meeting,

now approached the pair, and was introduced to the gentleman.   In a few moments
she returned to me, who had been regarding
the interview with silent amazement.

"It is Harvey Glade," she said,—"Kitty's
cousin.   We should invite him to stay here
to-night."

I cannot conceive of anything which more
quickly than these words would have snuffed
out the light which had illumined the
vision of my house with Kitty in it ; but it
was impossible for me to forget that I was
a gentleman and the master of Eastover,
and, instantly causing my perception of
these facts to take precedence of my gather-
ing emotions, I stepped up to Miss Kitty,
and, asking to be introduced to her cousin,
I begged him to make my house his home
during his stay in the neighbourhood.

This invitation was accepted, as I supposed it would be when I made it ; yet I
must own that I did not expect Mr. Glade
to remain at my house for a week.   Of
course his presence prevented the execution
of any of my plans regarding the promotion
of my intimacy with Kitty ; but although
the interruption caused me much vexation,
I maintained the equanimity due to my position, and hoped each day that the young

man would take his leave. Towards the end
of his visit I became aware, through the
medium of my sisters, to whom I had left
in a great degree the entertainment of our
guests, that young Glade was actually engaged to be married to Kitty. She had told
them so herself. This statement, which
chilled to the verge of frigidity my every
sensibility, was amplified as follows: The
young people had been attached to each
other for some time, but the visits of Glade
having been discouraged by Miss Kitty's
family, they had not seen each other lately,
and there had been no positive declaration
of amatory sentiment on the part of either.
But this protracted sojourn in my house had
given the young man all the opportunity he
could desire, and the matter was settled so
definitely that there was no reason to suppose that the better judgment of her elders
would cause the young woman to change her
mind.

Here was a fine ending to my endeavours
to assist my fate. Instead of so doing, I
had assisted the fate of Mr. Harvey Glade,
in whose welfare I had no interest whatever.
He had not known that Miss Kitty was
coming to my house; he had not even been
aware, until he met her at Eastover, that I

was acquainted with her family. Had it not been for my endeavours to promote my own fortune in the direction of the lady, he would have had no opportunity to make her his own ; and they probably would not have seen each other again, unless he had happened to call upon her as the mistress of Eastover. Instead of aiding Miss Kitty to enter my life on the 14th of September, I had ushered her into his life on the 16th of that month.

For a week after the departure of our guests—the young man went first—I found myself in a state of mental depression from which the kindly efforts of my sisters could not arouse me. Not only was I deeply chagrined at what had occurred, but it wounded my self-respect to think that my fate, which had been satisfactorily pursuing the course I had marked out for it, should have been thus suddenly and disastrously turned aside. I felt that I must confess myself conquered. It was an unusual and a difficult thing for me to do this, but there was no help for it. I took out my diary, and turned to the page whereon I had challenged fate. That entry must be erased. I must humble myself, and acknowledge it untrue.

At the moment that I dipped the pen in

the inkstand there was a knock at the door, and Grace Anna entered.

"I have just had a letter," she said, "from dear Jane Wiltby, who married your old schoolfellow, Dr. Tom. I thought you would like to hear the news it contains. They have a little girl, and she is to be named for me."

"How old is it?" I asked, with indifferent interest.

"She was born on the 14th of September," said Grace Anna.

I sat erect, and looked at my sister— looked at her without seeing her. Thoughts, like clouds upon the horizon brightened by the rays of dawn, piled themselves up in my mind. Dr. Tom, the companion of my youth, ever my cherished friend ! Jane, woman above women ! Grace Anna !

I laid down the pen, and, leaving the momentous and prognostic entry just as I had written it, I closed my diary, and placed it in my desk.

He who cannot adapt himself to the vagaries of a desired fate, who cannot place himself upon the road by which he expects it to come, and who cannot wait for it with cheerful confidence, is not worthy to be an assistant arbiter of his destiny.

II.

THE fact that on the day indicated in my diary a young creature not only came into my life, but into her own, greatly satisfied and encouraged me. I would begin at the beginning. Within the sphere of my immediate cognisance would grow and develop the infant, the child, the girl, the woman, and finally, the wife. What influence might I not have upon this development? The parents were my friends; the child was my selected bride. The possibilities of advantageous guidance, unseen perhaps, but potent to a degree unattainable by a mere parent or guardian, were, to my thinking, boundless.

I was now more content than I had been in the case of the young lady whom I had supposed had been given me by Fate, but who, it now appeared very fortunately, had been snatched away before my irrevocable mistake had been made. I was very grateful for this : I was grateful to Fate ; I was

grateful to Mr. Glade, the successful lover ;
I was even grateful to Kitty for not having
allowed herself to be influenced by anything she may have seen in me during our
short acquaintance. Of the past of Kitty I
knew little, as was well demonstrated by
the appearance of Harvey Glade. My
present *fiancée* had no past. With her and
with me it was all future, which would
gently crystallise, minute by minute and
day by day, into a present which would be
mutually our own.

Of course I said nothing of all this to any
one. The knowledge of our destiny was
locked up in the desk which held my diary
and in my own heart. When the proper
time came, she, first, should know. I am
an honourable man, and as such felt fully
qualified to be the custodian of what was,
in fact, her secret as well as mine.

I took an early opportunity to become acquainted with the one who was to be the
future partner of my life. It was towards
the end of October, I think, that I paid a
visit to Dr. Tom Wiltby and his wife Jane,
my predestined parents-in-law. Had they
known the position they occupied towards
me, they would have been a very much surprised couple. The interest I exhibited in

their first-born did, as I thought, surprise them a little, but it only increased the warmth of the welcome they gave me, and drew me closer to their hearts. The emotions which possessed me when, in the preceding summer, I had stood awaiting the moment when Kitty Watridge should enter the room and first present herself to my sight were nothing to those which quickened the action of my heart as a nurse brought into the Wiltby parlour a carefully disposed bundle of drapery, in the midst of which reposed my future wife.

I approached, and looked at her. Her face was displayed to view, but her form was undistinguishable. For an instant our eyes met; but, so far as I could judge, no spark of reciprocal sympathy seemed to shine from hers. In fact, they rolled about in an irrelevant manner which betokened a preoccupation so intense that even the advent of a husband could have no effect upon it. But whatever the child had on its mind —or stomach—gave a volcanic mobility to its countenance, which caused me much to wonder. The eyes then closed, and appeared to be writhing and swelling beneath their lids; the mouth was alternately convoluted and unrolled towards nose, cheeks,

and chin ; while the rest of the face, which
had been of an Indian reddish hue, now darkened, and from the puffy jaws to the top of
the bald head seemed moved by a spasm,
but whether of premonition or despair I
could not tell.

I withdrew my gaze.   It might be well
that I should wait for a time before allow-
ing my eyes to feed upon this countenance.

I went away a little disappointed.   The
chaoticness of initiatory existence had never
before been so forcibly impressed on my
mind.

During the following winter and spring I
built up an ideal, or rather a series of ideals.
They were little children, they were girls,
they were women.   At about nineteen years
of age the individual existence of each
ended, and became merged into the oneness
of my matrimonial life.   Sometimes my
ideal was a blonde, sometimes a brunette.
From the cursory glance I had had of the one
to whom all these fancies referred, I could
not judge whether she would be dark or
fair.   She had no hair, and all that I could
remember of her eyes was that they had no
soul light.   Her father was dark, her mother
fair : she might be either.

Of all the legendary heroines of love, none

ever so impressed me as that Francesca
whose strong love not only braved every
prejudice and barrier of earth, but, according to eye-witnesses of the fact, floated with
her indefinitely through hell. In verse and
picture, and upon the stage, I knew Francesca well,—better, perhaps, than any other
woman. But to such an one I would not be
merely a Paolo, but the elder brother also.
I would have no proxy, no secret love, no
unfaithfulness. There should be all the im-
petuosity, all the spirit of self-immolation,
without any necessity for it. She who was
to be mine had become in my thoughts a
Francesca, and she grew before my mind to
ripened loveliness. Her eyes sparkled with
rapture when, as through the gates of old
Ravenna, the fair Ghibelline first saw the
brave rider that she thought to wed, so this
one would see through the gates of womanly
consciousness, not a mere envoy, but both
Malatesta brothers in one,—lover and husband,—me. With such an imaginary one I
read legends of old loves; with such an one
I sat in shaded bowers, her young face upturned to mine, and the red light from the
wings touching with colour the passionate
picture. But no jester watched with sneer-
ing gibes, no husband fought afar on battle-

field; Paolo and Lanciotto in one looked into the uplifted eyes.

It was in the early summer that my two sisters and myself were invited to the Wiltby mansion for a visit, which our kindly hosts hoped would be somewhat pro-tracted. Among other things that were to be done the baby was to be baptized, and Grace Anna, for whom she was named, was to act as godmother. I was very glad to make this visit. Quite a long time had now elapsed since my first interview with Fran-cesca, as I always intended to call her, notwithstanding the name that might be bestowed upon her by the Church ; and she must have now begun to foreshadow, in a measure, that which she was to be.

When I saw her I found that there was not quite so much foreshadowing as I had expected ; but, in spite of that, she was a little creature whom, without doing violence to any æsthetic instinct, I could take to my heart. She was a pudgy infant, with blue eyes, a blankety head, and a mouth that was generally ready to break into a smile if you tickled the corners of it. Instead of the long and flowing draperies in which I first beheld her, she now wore short dresses, and that she possessed remarkably fat legs

and blue woollen socks was a fact which
Francesca never failed to endeavour to im-
press upon my observation. I excited a
great deal of surprise, with some admiration
on the part of the mother and occasional
jocular remarks from Bertha, my younger
sister, by showing, at the very beginning of
our visit, a strong preference for the society
of the baby. I asked to be allowed to take
her into my arms, and walk with her into
the garden; and although this privilege was
at first denied me, unless some lady should
accompany me, I being considered quite in-
experienced in the care of an infant, I at
last gained my point, and frequently had
the pleasure of a *tête-à-tête* stroll with Francesca. With my future bride in my arms,
slowly walking in the shaded avenues of
the garden, I gave my imagination full play.
I enlarged her eyes, and gave them a steadi-
ness of upturn which they did not now possess; the white fuzz upon her head grew
into rich masses of gold-brown hair; the
nose was lengthened and refined; her lips
were less protruded, and made more con-
tinuously dry; while a good deal of fatty
deposit was removed from the cheeks and
the second chin. As I walked thus tenderly
gazing down upon her, and often removing

her little fist from her mouth, I pictured in
her lineaments the budding womanhood for
which I waited. I would talk softly to her,
and although she seldom answered but in a
gurgling monotone I saw in our intercourse
the dawning of a unity to be.

After we had been a few days at the
Wiltby house Miss Kitty Watridge came
there, also on a visit. Her engagement to
Mr. Glade had not produced much effect
upon her personal appearance, although I
thought her something quieter, and with a
little sedateness which I had not observed
in her before. Her advent at this time was
not to my liking. As an object of my regard,
she had, in becoming engaged to another,
ceased to exist ; she had passed out of my
sphere of consideration, and the fact that she
had once acted a prominent part within it
made it appear to me that propriety de-
manded that she should not only go out of
it, but stay out of it. Her influence upon
my intercourse with Francesca was, from the
first, objectionable. My sisters had always
been accustomed to regard my wishes with a
gratifying respect, and Mrs. Wiltby seemed
anxious to imitate them in this laudable
action. But Miss Watridge had apparently
no such ideas, and she showed this most ob-

jectionably by imagining that she had as
much right to the baby as I had.   Of course
she could not understand how matters stood,
—nobody but myself could understand that ;
but she had not the native delicacy of perception of my sisters and Jane Wiltby. She
could not know in how many ways she interfered with my desires and purposes. My
morning walks were, in a manner, broken
up ; for sometimes the new-comer actually
insisted upon carrying the baby herself, in
which case I retired, and sought some other
promenade.   But after a few days I found
that the indulgence of any resentment of
this sort not only made me the object of remark, but promised to entirely break up my
plans in regard to Francesca.   I wished to
create in my mind while here such an image
of her, matured and perfected according to
my own ideas, that I could live and com-
mune with her during the absences, more or
less protracted, which must intervene before
the day when I should take her wholly to
myself.   As I could not expect to stay here
very much longer, I must not lose what
opportunities I had, and so concluded to
resume my walks with Francesca, even if
Miss Watridge should sometimes intrude
herself upon us.

I must admit, however, that this she did not do, considering the matter with strict regard to fact. She generally possessed herself of the baby, and if I wished its company I was obliged to intrude myself upon her. The plan I now adopted was, I think, somewhat ingenious. As is my wont, I endeavoured to shape to my advantage this obstacle which I now found in my way. My intercourse with Francesca had not been altogether satisfactory. For one thing, there had been too much unity about it. A certain degree of this was, indeed, desirable, but I was obliged to be, at once, not only husband and lover, but lady also ; for Francesca gave me no help in this regard, except, perchance, an occasional look of entreaty, which might as well mean that she would like a bottle of milk as that she yearned for fond communion of the soul. When I addressed her as my developed ideal I imagined her answers, and so continued the gentle conversation ; but, although she always spoke as I would wish, there were absent from our converse certain desirable elements which might have been looked for from the presence of a second intellect. Another source of dissatisfaction was that in many of our interviews Francesca acted in a manner which was not only disturbing, but indecorous. Frequently, when I was speaking with her on such subjects as foreign travel, when we two would wander amid the misty purples of Caprian sunsets, or stand together in vast palaces of hoarded art, she would struggle so convulsively, and throw upward with such violence her small blue socks, that, for the time, I wished she was swaddled and bound in the manner of the Della Robbia babies on the front of the Foundling Asylum in Florence.

A plan of relieving myself from the obvious disadvantages of my present method of intercourse with an intellect, a soul, and a person, which to be suitable for my companionship must necessarily be projected into the future, now suggested itself to me. If Miss Watridge persisted in forcing herself upon Francesca, she might at least make herself useful by taking the place of that young person so far as regarded a part in the conversation. Her entity occupied a position in respect to growth and development which was about the same as that to which I was in the habit of projecting Francesca. Her answers to my remarks would be analogous, if not similar, to those which might be expected from the baby when she arrived at maturity. Thus, in a manner, I could talk to Francesca, and receive her answers from the lips of Miss Kitty. This would be as truly love-making by proxy as when the too believing Lanciotto sent from Rimini his younger brother to bear to him Ravenna's pearl. But here was no guile, no dishonesty; the messenger, the vehicle, the interpreter, in this case, knew nothing of the feelings now in action, or to be set in action, of the principals in the affair. She did not know, indeed, that there were two principals. As far as she herself was concerned, she had, and could have, no interest in the matter. She was engaged to be married to Mr. Glade, which, in my eyes, was the same thing as being already married to him; and any thoughts or mental emotions that she might have relating to affectionate interest in one of the opposite sex would of course be centred in Mr. Glade. With Francesca and myself she would have nothing to do but unconsciously to assist in the transmission of sentiment. Had Paolo been engaged to marry a suitable young person before he started for Ravenna, it is probable that the limited partnership which Dante noticed in the Inferno would never have been formed.

It was by slow degrees, and with a good

deal of caution, that I began my new course
of action.   Taking the child in my arms, I
invited Miss Watridge to accompany us in
our walk.   Thus, together, we slowly strolled
along the garden avenue, shaded by the fresh
greenness of June foliage, and flecked here
and there by patches of sunlight, which
moved upon the gravel in unison with the
gentle breeze.   Our conversation, at first
relating to simple and everyday matters,
was soon directed by me into a channel in
which I could perceive whether or not I
should succeed in this project of representative rejoinder.   It was not long before I was
pleased to discover that the mind of the
young lady was of as good natural quality
and as well cultivated as I had formerly supposed it to be ; having then little upon which
to base my judgment, except the general impression which her personality had made upon
me.   That impression having been entirely
effaced, I was enabled with clearer vision and
sounder judgment to determine the value of
her mental exhibit.   I found that she had
read with some discrimination, and with a
tendency to independent thought she united
a becoming respect for the opinions of those
who, by reason of superior years, experience,
and sex, might be supposed to move on a

psychological plane somewhat higher than her own. These were dispositions the development of which I hoped to assist in the young Francesca, and it may be imagined that I was much gratified to find my model so closely resembling that personality which I wished, in a manner, to create.

Thus, up and down, daily, would we stroll and talk. With the real Francesca on my arm, sometimes sleeping, and sometimes indulging in disturbing muscular exercises, which I gently endeavoured to restrain, I addressed myself to my ideal Francesca, an aerial maiden, garbed in simple robes of white touched by a soft suggestion of Italian glow, and ever with tender eyes upturned to mine; while from her proxy, walking by my side, came to me the thoughts and sentiments of her fresh young heart.

It was quite natural that I should be more interested in a conversation of this kind than in one in which I was obliged to supply the remarks on either side. To be sure, in the latter case there was a unison of thought between myself and the ideal Francesca that was very satisfactory, but which lacked the piquancy given by unexpectedness of reply and the interest consequent upon gentle argument.

It so happened that the morning occupations of Mrs. Wiltby and my sisters were those in which Miss Watridge did not care to join, and thus she was commonly left free to make one of the company of four which took its morning walks upon the garden avenue.   I imagined that she supposed it was generally thought that she was taking care of the baby and affording it advantages of outdoor air, in the performance of which pleasing duty my presence was so unnecessary that the probability of it was not even considered.   Thus it was that upon every fair day—and all those days were fair—our morning strolls were prolonged for an hour or more, generally terminated only by the culminating resolve of Francesca to attract to herself so much attention that a return to the house was necessary.   It may be supposed that it would have been better to have eliminated the element of the actual being from the female side of our little company.   But that side, several as it was in its component personages, represented to me the one Francesca ; and had I not held and felt the presence of the actual living creature, who was to be and to say all that my mind saw and my ear heard, I could not have spoken as I wished to speak to the ideality who was to be my wife when it became a reality. The conjunction seemed to me a perfect one, and under the circumstances I could wish for nothing better.

As our acquaintance ripened and mellowed in the pleasant summer days, I was enabled to see more clearly into the soul and heart of the Francesca that was to be, looking at them through the transparent mind of Miss Kitty Watridge. According to the pursuance of my plan, I gradually, and as far as possible imperceptibly, changed the nature of our converse. From talking of the material world, and those objects in it which had pleased our vision or excited reflection, we passed to the consideration, very cursory at first, of those sentiments which appear to emanate from ourselves without the aid of extraneous agency. Then, by slow degrees, the extraneous agency was allowed to enter upon the scene, coming in so quietly that at first it was scarcely noticeable. The dependence of man upon man was discussed, not only for material good, but for intellectual support and comfort. Then, following a course not exactly in accordance with that of nature, but which suited my purposes, we spoke of social ties,—of the friendships which spring up here and there from these ; of the natural affections of the family ; and, finally, the subject arising in consistent se- quence, of that congruent intermental action of the intellect of two persons, generally male and female, who frequently, without family ties of any kind and but little pre- vious acquaintanceship, find, each in the other, an adaptiveness of entity which is mutually satisfactory.

The vicarious replies of Francesca were, in almost every instance, all that I could have wished. Sometimes there were symp- toms of hesitancy or reluctance in the enun- ciation of what was, obviously, the suitable reply to some of my remarks in regard to the deeper sentiments ; but, on the whole, had the ideal lady of my love spoken to me, her words could not have better aroused my every sentiment of warm regard.

Sometimes I wondered, as thus we walked and talked, what Mr. Glade would think about it if he could see us so much together, and listen to our converse. But this thought I put aside as unworthy of me. It was an insult to myself as an honourable man ; it was an uncalled-for aspersion on Miss Wat- ridge, and a stain upon my idealistic inter- course with Francesca. If Mr. Glade was coarse and vulgar enough to interject his personality into this perfectly working system of intellectual action, from which the individuality of Miss Watridge was entirely eliminated, her part in it being merely to represent another, I could not help it. It was this consciousness of rectitude, this probity of purpose, which raised our little drama so far above the level of the old story of the wedded Guelph and Ghibelline.

With my mind satisfied on this subject, I did not hesitate, when the proper time seemed to have arrived, to allow myself to imagine Francesca at the age of nineteen. I could not much longer remain in this place, as we had now overstayed the original limit of our visit ; and there was danger, too, that Miss Watridge might be called away. I wished, while the opportunity continued, to develop the imaginary life of Francesca into perfect womanhood, so that I could carry away with me an image of my future wife, which I could set upon the throne of my affection, there to be revered, cherished, and guarded, until the time came when the real Francesca should claim the seat. Of course, under these circumstances, a certain fervour of thought and expression was not only necessary, but excusable, and

I did not scruple to allow it to myself.
Always with the real Francesca in my arms,
in order that even my own superconscien-
tiousness might not take me to task, I de-
livered my sentiments without drawing the
veil of precautionary expression over their
amatory significance. It was at this stage
of our intercourse that I asked Miss Watridge to allow me to call her Francesca ; for
it was only by so doing that I could fully
identify her voice with that of the visionary
creature who was now exciting the stirring
impulses of my heart. When she asked me
why I wished to call her by this name, I
could only tell her that it was for ideal purposes ; and without making further inquiries,
she consented that I should use it—for the
present. As it was only for the present
that I thought of so doing, this much of
acquiescence was sufficient, and I called her
by the name I loved.

The softly spoken, well-considered replies, the gentle ejaculations, and the de-
mure but earnest attention which my speech
elicited well befitted the fairest vision of
pure young womanhood that my soul could
call before me. But, notwithstanding this,
there was something wanting. I longed for
the upturned eyes, ever fixed upon my own,

of the Francesca of the stage. I longed for the fair white hands clasped and trembling as I spoke. I longed for that intensity of soul-merge in which the loved one breathes and lives only that she may hear the words I speak, and watch the thoughts that fashion in my face. Without all this I could never take away with me the image of the true Francesca. Without this there would be wanting, in the fair conception, that artistic roundness, that completeness of outline and purpose, which would satisfy the exigencies of my nature. I could not consent to carry with me for years an ideal existence, incomplete, imperfected,—a statue devoid of those last touches of the master which make it seem to live.

Therefore I sought, with much earnestness and fixity of intention, to call up the last element needed to complete that lovely creation which was to be my companion through the years of waiting for the real Francesca. It was a great comfort and support to me to reflect that I could do this with such safety, with such unusual advantages. I addressed myself to no being in existence. Even the little creature on my arm, who had fallen into a habit of dozing when not noticed, and to whom belonged, in fact, my every gift and legacy of love, was not of age to come into her fortune, nor could her infantile mind be injured by its contemplation. And as for Miss Watridge, she, as I continually repeated to myself, was acting simply as the representative of another, and her real self was not concerned in the little drama, in which she did not even take a part; merely assuming, as in a rehearsal, a character which another actor, not able then to be present, would play in the actual performance.

It was the loveliest morning of all the summer that I made my supreme effort. At the very bottom of the garden was a little arbour of honeysuckles. No crimson stage-light shone in upon it, but the sunbeams pushed their way here and there through the screen of leaves, and brightened the interior with points of light. It was a secluded spot, to which I had never yet led my companions, for the period had not before arrived for such sequesterment. But now we sat down here upon a little bench : I at one end, the young Francesca on my knee, and Miss Watridge at my left. In the place where this lady sat also sat the ideal Francesca, occupying the same space, and endowed, for the time, with the same form and features. It

was to this being that I now addressed my
fervid words; low-burning, it is true, but
alive with all the heat and glow that pre-
cedes blaze. I told a tale; not reading
from pages of mediæval script the legend
of the love of Launcelot and Queen Guin-
evere, as does Paolo in the play, but relating a story which was a true one, for it was
my own. I spoke as I expected to speak
some day to the little creature on my knee.
Taking with my disengaged hand that of
the lady by my side, I said that which
raised a lovely countenance to mine, that
showed me the beauty of her upturned eyes;
and as I looked and spoke I felt that the
very pulses of her soul were throbbing in
accord with mine. Here was enacting in
very truth the scene I had viewed upon the
stage, and which so often since had risen
before my fancy. Possessed by the spirit
of this scene, carried onward by that same
tide of passional emotion the gradual rise
of which it had portrayed, I gave myself
up to its influences, and acted it out unto
its very culmination. I stooped, and, in
the words of the Arthurian legend, "I
kissed her full upon the mouth."

Swift as the sudden fall of summer rain,
I felt the wild abandonment of clinging arms

about my neck, of tears upon my face that
were not mine, of words of love that I spoke
not; and it came to me like a flash that
she who clung to me, and around whom my
arm was passed, was Kitty Watridge, and
not a visionary Ghibelline.

In the midst of my varying emotions I
clasped closer to me the real Francesca,
who thereupon gave vent to her feelings
by parting wide her toothless gums, and
filling the summer air with a long yell.
At this rude interruption, the arms fell
from my neck, and the face was quickly
withdrawn from mine.

Now came hurrying steps upon the gravel
walk, and my sister Bertha ran in upon us.
"What on earth are you doing to that
baby?" she cried. She snatched the child
from me, and then stood astonished, gazing
first at me and then at Kitty, who had
started to her feet, with sparkling tears still
in her eyes and a sunset glow upon her
face. Without a word, the wicked Bertha
laughed a little laugh, and, folding the
child within her arms, she ran away.

I sat speechless for a moment, and then
I turned to Kitty; but she, too, had gone,
having fled in another direction. I was left
alone : gone was the real Francesca ; gone

was the fair ideal; gone was Kitty. I stood
bewildered, and, in a manner, dazed. I felt
as if I had fallen from the fourteenth century
into the nineteenth, and that the shock had
hurt me. I felt, too, a sense of culpability,
as if I had been somewhere where I had no
right to be; as if I had been a trespasser, a
poacher, an intruder upon the times or on
the rights of others. The fact that I was a
strictly honourable man, scorning perfidy in
its every form, made my feelings the more
poignant. A little reflection helped me to
understand it all. I had carried out my plan
so carefully, with such regard to its gradual
development, that by degrees Miss Watridge
had grown into the ideal Francesca, and had
to all intents and purposes gone back with
me into the Middle Ages, in order to better
portray my perfected ideal. The baby sitting on my right knee, while a future stage
of her life was being personated by the lady
at my side, might belong to any age; there
was nothing incongruous in her presence on
the scene. It was the entrance of my sister
Bertha that broke the spell, that shattered
the whole fabric I had so elaborately built.
She was of the present, of to-day, of the
exact second, in which she helped anything
to happen. An impersonation of the Now,

her coming banished every idea of the Past or Future.

Like an actor in a play, on whom his everyday clothes and the broad light of day have suddenly fallen, I walked slowly to the house. Meeting my older sister, Grace Anna, near the door, I took her aside, and said to her, "When is Mr. Glade expected here?"

"What for?" she asked, with eyes dilated.

"To marry Kitty Watridge," said I.

"What do you mean?" exclaimed my sister. "That match was broken off last winter."

It may well be supposed that, remembering what Bertha had seen, and doubtless imagined; that remembering what Kitty had done and said; and recalling, too, how I felt when she did it and said it, I resolved, instead of waiting eighteen long years for another, to accept as the Francesca of my dreams, and as the veritable wife of my actual existence, this dear girl, who was able to represent at this very present the every attribute and quality of my ideal woman.

In the autumn we were married. Thus my Fate, disclaiming my efforts to assist it, no matter in what direction, rose dominant, and, attending to my affairs in its own way, gave me Kitty at last.

But I shall always feel sorry for the baby.

THE DISCOURAGER OF
HESITANCY.

THE DISCOURAGER OF HESITANCY.

IT was nearly a year after the occurrence of that event in the arena of the semi-barbaric King known as the incident of the lady or the tiger, that there came to the palace of this monarch a deputation of five strangers from a far country. These men, of venerable and dignified aspect and demeanour, were received by a high officer of the court, and to him they made known their errand.

"Most noble officer," said the speaker of the deputation, "it so happened that one of our countrymen was present here, in your capital city, on that momentous occasion when a young man who had dared to aspire to the hand of your King's daughter had been placed in the arena, in the midst of the assembled multitude, and ordered to open

237

one of two doors, not knowing whether a ferocious tiger would spring out upon him, or a beauteous lady would advance, ready to become his bride. Our fellow-citizen who was then present was a man of super-sensitive feelings, and at the moment when the youth was about to open the door he was so fearful lest he should behold a horrible spectacle, that his nerves failed him, and he fled precipitately from the arena, and mounting his camel rode homeward as fast as he could go.

"We were all very much interested in the story which our countryman told us, and we were extremely sorry that he did not wait to see the end of the affair. We hoped, however, that in a few weeks some traveller from your city would come among us and bring us further news; but up to the day when we left our country, no such traveller had arrived. At last it was determined that the only thing to be done was to send a deputation to this country, and to ask the question: 'Which came out of the open door, the lady, or the tiger?'"

When the high officer had heard the mission of this most respectable deputation, he led the five strangers into an inner room, where they were seated upon soft cushions, and where he ordered coffee, pipes, sherbet, and other semi-barbaric refreshments to be served to them ; then, taking his seat before them, he thus addressed the visitors—

" Most noble strangers, before answering the question you have come so far to ask, I will relate to you an incident which occurred not very long after that to which you have referred. It is well known in all regions hereabouts that our great King is very fond of the presence of beautiful women about his court. All the ladies-in-waiting upon the Queen and Royal Family are most lovely maidens, brought here from every part of the kingdom. The fame of this concourse of beauty, unequalled in any other royal court, has spread far and wide ; and had it not been for the equally widespread fame of the systems of impetuous justice adopted by our King, many foreigners would doubtless have visited our court.

" But not very long ago there arrived here from a distant land a prince of distin-guished appearance and undoubted rank. To such an one, of course, a royal audience was granted, and our King met him very graciously, and begged him to make known the object of his visit. Thereupon the Prince informed his Royal Highness that, having heard of the superior beauty of the ladies of his court, he had come to ask permission to make one of them his wife.

"When our King heard this bold announcement, his face reddened, he turned uneasily on his throne, and we were all in dread lest some quick words of furious condemnation should leap from out his quivering lips. But by a mighty effort he controlled himself; and after a moment s silence he turned to the Prince, and said: 'Your request is granted. To-morrow at noon you shall wed one of the fairest damsels of our court.' Then turning to his officers, he said: 'Give orders that everything be prepared for a wedding in this palace at high noon to-morrow. Convey this royal Prince to suitable apartments. Send to him tailors, boot-makers, hatters, jewellers, armourers; men of every craft, whose services he may need. Whatever he asks, provide. And let all be ready for the ceremony to-morrow.'

"'But, your Majesty,' exclaimed the Prince, 'before we make these preparations, I would like——'

"'Say no more!' roared the King. 'My royal orders have been given, and nothing more is needed to be said. You asked a boon; I granted it; and I will hear no more on the subject. Farewell, my Prince, until to-morrow noon.'

"At this the King arose, and left the audience chamber, while the Prince was hurried away to the apartments selected for him. And here came to him tailors, hatters, jewellers, and every one who was needed to fit him out in grand attire for the wedding. But the mind of the Prince was much troubled and perplexed.

"'I do not understand,' he said to his attendants, 'this precipitancy of action. When am I to see the ladies, that I may choose among them? I wish opportunity, not only to gaze upon their forms and faces, but to become acquainted with their relative intellectual development.'

"'We can tell you nothing,' was the answer. 'What our King thinks right, that will he do. And more than this we know not.'

"'His Majesty's notions seem to be very peculiar,' said the Prince, 'and, so far as I can see, they do not at all agree with mine.'

"At that moment an attendant whom the Prince had not noticed before came and stood beside him. This was a broad-shouldered man of cheery aspect, who car-

ried, its hilt in his right hand, and its broad
back resting on his broad arm, an enormous
scimitar, the upturned edge of which was
keen and bright as any razor. Holding this
formidable weapon as tenderly as though it
had been a sleeping infant, this man drew
closer to the Prince and bowed.

"'Who are you?' exclaimed his Highness, starting back at the sight of the
frightful weapon.

"'I,' said the other, with a courteous
smile, 'am the Discourager of Hesitancy.
When our King makes his wishes known to
any one, a subject or visitor, whose disposition in some little points may be supposed
not to wholly coincide with that of his
Majesty, I am appointed to attend him
closely, that should he think of pausing in
the path of obedience to the royal will, he
may look at me, and proceed.'

"The Prince looked at him, and proceeded to be measured for a coat.

"The tailors and shoemakers and hatters
worked all night; and the next morning,
when everything was ready, and the hour
of noon was drawing nigh, the Prince again
anxiously inquired of his attendants when
he might expect to be introduced to the
ladies.

" 'The King will attend to that,' they said. ' We know nothing of the matter.'

" ' Your Highness,' said the Discourager of Hesitancy, approaching with a courtly bow, ' will observe the excellent quality of this edge.' And drawing a hair from his head, he dropped it upon the upturned edge of his scimitar, upon which it was cut in two at the moment of touching.

" The Prince glanced and turned upon his heel.

" Now came officers to conduct him to the grand hall of the palace, in which the ceremony was to be performed. Here the Prince found the King seated on the throne, with his nobles, his courtiers, and his officers standing about him in magnificent array. The Prince was led to a position in front of the King, to whom he made obeisance, and then said—

" ' Your Majesty, before I proceed further——'

" At this moment an attendant, who had approached with a long scarf of delicate silk, wound it about the lower part of the Prince's face so quickly and adroitly that he was obliged to cease speaking. Then, with wonderful dexterity, the rest of the scarf was wound around the Prince's head, so that he was completely blindfolded. Thereupon the attendant quickly made openings in the scarf over the mouth and ears, so that the Prince might breathe and hear; and fastening the ends of the scarf securely, he retired.

"The first impulse of the Prince was to snatch the silken folds from his head and face; but as he raised his hands to do so, he heard beside him the voice of the Discourager of Hesitancy, who gently whispered: 'I am here, your Highness.' And, with a shudder, the arms of the Prince fell down by his side.

"Now before him he heard the voice of a priest, who had begun the marriage service in use in that semi-barbaric country. At his side he could hear a delicate rustle, which seemed to proceed from fabrics of soft silk. Gently putting forth his hand, he felt folds of such silk close beside him. Then came the voice of the priest requesting him to take the hand of the lady by his side; and reaching forth his right hand, the Prince received within it another hand so small, so soft, so delicately fashioned, and so delightful to the touch, that a thrill went through his being. Then, as was the custom of the country, the priest first asked the lady would she have this man to be her husband. To which the answer gently came in the sweetest voice he ever heard : 'I will.'

"Then ran raptures rampant through the Prince's blood. The touch, the tone, enchanted him. All the ladies of that court were beautiful ; the Discourager was behind him ; and through his parted scarf he boldly answered : 'Yes, I will.'

"Whereupon the priest pronounced them man and wife.

"Now the Prince heard a bustle about him ; the long scarf was rapidly unrolled from his head ; and he turned, with a start, to gaze upon his bride. To his utter amazement, there was no one there. He stood alone. Unable on the instant to ask a question or say a word, he gazed blankly about him.

"Then the King arose from his throne, and came down, and took him by the hand.

"'Where is my wife?' gasped the Prince.

"'She is here,' said the King, leading him to a curtained doorway at the side of the hall.

"The curtains were drawn aside, and the Prince, entering, found himself in a long apartment, near the opposite wall of which stood a line of forty ladies, all dressed in rich attire, and each one apparently more beautiful than the rest.

"Waving his hand towards the line, the King said to the Prince: 'There is your bride! Approach, and lead her forth! But remember this: that if you attempt to take away one of the unmarried damsels of our court, your execution shall be instantaneous. Now, delay no longer. Step up and take your bride.'

"The Prince, as in a dream, walked slowly along the line of ladies, and then walked slowly back again. Nothing could he see about any one of them to indicate that she was more of a bride than the others. Their dresses were all similar; they all blushed; they all looked up, and then looked down. They all had charming little hands. Not one spoke a word. Not one lifted a finger to make a sign. It was evident that the orders given them had been very strict.

"'Why this delay?' roared the King. 'If I had been married this day to one so fair as the lady who wedded you, I should not wait one second to claim her.'

"The bewildered Prince walked again up and down the line. At this time there was a slight change in the countenances of two of the ladies. One of the fairest gently smiled as he passed her. Another, just as beautiful, slightly frowned.

" 'Now,' said the Prince to himself, 'I am sure that it is one of those two ladies whom I have married. But which? One smiled. And would not any woman smile when she saw, in such a case, her husband coming towards her? But, then, were she not his bride, would she not smile with satisfaction to think he had not selected her, and that she had not led him to an untimely doom? Then again, on the other hand, would not any woman frown when she saw her husband come towards her and fail to claim her? Would she not knit her lovely brows? And would she not inwardly say, "It is I! Don't you know it? Don't you feel it? Come!" But if this woman had not been married, would she not frown when she saw the man looking at her? Would she not say to herself, "Don't stop at me! It is the next but one. It is two ladies above. Go on!" And then again, the one who married me did not see my face. Would she not smile if she thought me comely? While if I wedded the one who frowned, could she restrain her disapprobation if she did not like me? Smiles invite the approach of true

love. A frown is a reproach to a tardy advance. A smile——'

" 'Now, hear me !' loudly cried the King.
'In ten seconds, if you do not take the lady
we have given you, she, who has just been
made your bride, shall be your widow.'

"And, as the last word was uttered,
the Discourager of Hesitancy stepped close
behind the Prince, and whispered : 'I am
here !'

"Now the Prince could not hesitate an
instant ; and he stepped forward and took
one of the two ladies by the hand.

"Loud rang the bells ; loud cheered the
people ; and the King came forward to con-
gratulate the Prince. He had taken his
lawful bride.

"Now, then," said the high officer to the
deputation of five strangers from a far country, "When you can decide among yourselves which lady the prince chose, the one
who smiled or the one who frowned, then
will I tell you which came out of the open
door, the lady or the tiger !"

At the latest accounts the five strangers
had not yet decided.

OUR STORY.

OUR STORY.

I.

I BECAME acquainted with Miss Bessie Vancouver at a reception given by an eminent literary gentleman in New York. The circumstances were a little peculiar. Miss Vancouver and I had each written and recently published a book; and we were introduced to each other as young authors whose works had made us known to the public, and who, consequently, should know each other. The peculiarity of the situation lay in the fact that I had not read Miss Vancouver's book, nor had she read mine. Consequently, although each felt bound to speak of the work of the other, neither of us could do it except in the most general and cautious way. I was quite sure that her book was a novel, but that was all that I knew about it, except that I had heard it well spoken of; but she supposed my book was of a scientific character, whereas, in reality, it also was a novel, although its title did not indicate the fact. There was

251

therefore an air of restraint and stiffness
about our first interview which it might not
have had if we had frankly acknowledged
our shortcomings. But, as the general conversation led her to believe that she was the
only person in the room who had not read
my book, and me to believe that I was the
only one who had not read hers, we were
naturally loathe to confess the truth to each
other.

I next met Miss Vancouver in Paris, at
the house of a lady whose parlours are the
frequent rendezvous of Americans, especially those given to art or literature. This
time we met on different ground. I had
read her book and she mine; and as soon
as we had shaken hands we began to talk
of each other's work, not as if it had been
the beginning of a new conversation, but
rather as the continuation of one broken off.
Each liked the book of the other extremely,
and we were free to say so.

"But I am not satisfied with my novel,"
said Miss Vancouver. "There is too much
oneness about it; by which I mean that it
is not diversified enough. It is all, or nearly
all, about two people, who, of course, have
but one object in life; and it seems to me
now that their story might have been fin-

ished a great deal sooner, though, of course, in that case it would not have been long enough to make a book."

To this I politely answered that I did not agree with her, for the story was interesting to the very end; but, of course, if she had put more characters into it, and they had been as good in their way as those she already had, the book would have been that much the better. "As for me," I continued, "my trouble is entirely the other way. I have no oneness whatever. My tendency is much more to fifteen- or twenty-ness. I carry a story a little way in one direction, and then I stop and go off in another. It is sometimes difficult to make it understood why a character should have been brought into the story at all; and I have had a good deal of trouble in making some of them do something toward the end to show that they are connected with the general plot."

She said she had noticed that there was a wideness of scope in my book; but what she would have said further I do not know, for our hostess now came down upon us and carried off Miss Vancouver to introduce her to an old lady who had successfully steered about fifty barques across that sea on which Miss Vancouver had just set out.

Our next meeting was in a town on the Mediterranean, in the south of France. I had secured board at a large *pension* there, and was delighted to find that Miss Bessie Vancouver and her mother were already inmates of the house. As soon as I had the opportunity, I broached to her an idea which had frequently possessed my mind since our conversation in Paris. I proposed that we should write a story together, something like Erckmann-Chatrian, or Mark Twain and Mr. Warner in *The Gilded Age*. Since she had too much unity of purpose and travelled in too narrow a path, and I branched off too much, and had too great a tendency to variety, our styles, if properly blended, would possess all the qualities needed in a good story; and there was no reason why we should not, writing thus together, achieve a success greater, perhaps, than either of us could expect writing alone. I had thought so much on this subject that I was able to say a great deal, and to say it pretty well, too, so far as I could judge. Miss Vancouver listened with great attention, and the more I said, the more the idea pleased her. She said she would take the afternoon to consider the matter; and in the evening she told me in the parlour that she

had made up her mind, if I still thought
well of the plan, to assist me in writing a
story,—this being the polite way in which
she chose to put it,—but that she thought
it would be better for us to begin with a
short story, and not with a book, for in this
way we could sooner see how we would be
likely to succeed. Of course I agreed to
this proposition, and we arranged that we
should meet the next morning in the garden
and lay out a plan for our story.

The garden attached to the house in which
we lived was a very quaint and pleasant one.
It had been made a hundred years ago or
more by an Italian nobleman, whose mansion, now greatly altered, had become our
present *pension.* The garden was laid out
in a series of terraces on the side of a hill,
and abounded in walks shaded by orange
and lemon trees, arbours, and vine-covered
trellises; fountains, half concealed by over-
hanging ivy; and suddenly discovered stair-
ways, wide and shadowy, leading up into
regions of greater quaintness and seclusion.
Flowers were here, and palm-trees, and
great cactus-bushes, with their red fruit
half hollowed out by the nibbling birds.
From the upper terraces we could see the
blue Mediterranean spreading far away on

one side, while the snow-covered tops of
the maritime Alps stood bright against the
sky. The garden was little frequented, and
altogether it was a good place in which to
plan a story.

We consulted together for several days
before we actually began to work. At first,
we sat in an arbour on one of the lower
terraces, where there were a little iron table
and some chairs; but now and then a person would come there for a morning stroll,
and so we moved up higher to a seat under
a palm-tree, and the next day to another
terrace, where there was a secluded corner
overshadowed by huge cacti. But the place
which suited us best of all was the top of
an old tower at one end of the garden.
This tower had been built many, many hundred years before the garden was thought
of, and its broad, flat roof was level with
one of the higher terraces. Here we could
work and consult in quiet, with little fear
of being disturbed.

Not finding it easy to plan out the whole
story at once, we determined to begin by
preparing backgrounds. We concluded that
as this was to be a short story, it would be
sufficient to have descriptions of two natural
scenes in which the two principal incidents

should occur; and as we wished to do all our work from natural models, we thought it best to describe the scene which lay around us, than which nothing could be more beautiful or more suitable. One scene was to be on the sea-shore, with a mellow light upon the rippling waves, and the sails of fishing-vessels in the distance. This Miss Vancouver was to do, while I was to take a scene among the hills and mountains at the back of the town. I walked over there one afternoon when Miss Vancouver had gone out with her mother. I got on a high point, and worked up a very satisfactory description of the frowning mountains behind me, the old monasteries on the hills, and the town stretching out below, with a little river rushing along between two rows of picturesque washerwomen to the sea.

We read our backgrounds to each other, and were both very well satisfied. Our styles were as different as the scenes we described. Hers was clear and smooth, and mine forcible and somewhat abrupt, and thus the strong points of each scene were better brought out; but, in order that our styles might be unified, so to speak, by being judiciously blended, I suggested some strong and effective points to be introduced into her description, while she toned down some of my phrases, and added a word here and there which gave a colour and beauty to the description which it had not possessed before.

Our backgrounds being thus satisfactory, —and it took a good deal of consultation to make them so,—our next work was to provide characters for the story. These were to be drawn from life, for it would be perfectly ridiculous to create imaginary characters when there were so many original and interesting personages around us. We soon agreed upon an individual who would serve as a model for our hero ; I forget whether it was I or Miss Vancouver who first suggested him. He was a young man, but not so very young either, who lived in the house with us, and about whom there was a mystery. Nobody knew exactly who he was, or where he came from, or why he was here. It was evident he did not come for society, for he kept very much to himself; and the attractions of the town could not have brought him here, for he seemed to care very little about them. We seldom saw him except at the table and occasionally in the garden. When we met him in the latter place, he always seemed anxious to avoid observation; and as we did not wish to hurt his feelings by letting him suppose that he was an object of curiosity to us, we endeavoured, as far as possible, to make it apparent that we were not looking at him or thinking of him. But still, whenever we had a good chance, we studied him. Of course, we could not make out his mystery, but that was not necessary, nor did we, indeed, think it would be proper. We could draw him as we saw him, and then make the mystery what we pleased; its character depending a good deal upon the plot we devised.

Miss Vancouver undertook to draw the hero, and she went to work upon him immediately. In personal appearance, she altered the model a good deal. She darkened his hair, and took off his whiskers, leaving him only a moustache. She thought, too, that he ought to be a little taller, and asked me my height, which is five feet nine. She considered that a very good height, and brought the hero up to it. She also made him some years younger, but endeavoured, as far as seemed suitable to the story, to draw him exactly as he was.

I was to do the heroine, but found it very hard to choose a model. As I said before, we determined to draw all our characters from life, but I could think of no one, in the somewhat extensive company by which we were surrounded, who would answer my purpose. Nor could I fix my mind upon any person in other parts of the world, whom I knew or had known, who resembled the idea I had formed of our heroine. After thinking this matter over a good deal, I told Miss Vancouver that I believed the best thing I could do would be to take her for my model. I was with her a good deal, and thus could study out and work up certain points as I wrote, which would be a great advantage. She objected to this, because, as she said, the author of a story should not be drawn as its heroine. But I asserted that this would not be the case. She would merely suggest the heroine to me, and I would so do my work that the heroine would not suggest her to anybody else. This, I thought, was the way in which a model ought to be used. After we had talked the subject over a good deal, she agreed to my plan, and I went to work with much satisfaction. I gave no definite description of the lady, but endeavoured to indicate the impression which her person and character produced upon me. As such impressions are seldom the same in any two cases, there was no danger that my description could be referred back to her.

When I read to her the sketch I had written, she objected to parts of it as not being correct; but as I asserted that it was not intended as an exact copy of the model, she could not say it was not a true picture; and so, with some slight modifications, we let it stand. I thought myself that it was a very good piece of work. To me it seemed very lifelike and piquant, and I believed that other people would think it so.

We were now ready for the incidents and the plot, but at this point we were somewhat interrupted by Mrs. Vancouver. She came to me one morning, when I was waiting to go with her daughter to our study in the garden, and told me that she was very sorry to notice that Miss Vancouver and I had attracted attention to ourselves by being so much together; and, while she understood the nature of the literary labour on which we were engaged, she did not wish her daughter to become the object of general attention and remark in a foreign *pension*. I was very angry when I heard that people had been directing upon us their impertinent curiosity, and I discoursed warmly upon the subject.

" Where is the good," I said, "of a person
or persons devoting himself or themselves,
with enthusiasm and earnestness, to his or
their life-work, if he or they.are to be interfered with by the impertinent babble of the
multitude ? "

Mrs. Vancouver was not prepared to give
an exact answer to this question, but she
considered the babble of the multitude a
very serious thing.   She had been talking
to her daughter on the subject, and thought
it right to speak to me.

That morning we worked separately in
our rooms, but we accomplished little or
nothing.   It was, of course, impossible to do
anything of importance in a work of this
kind without consultation and co-operation.
The next day, however, I devised a plan
which would enable us, I thought, to pursue
our labours without attracting attention ;
and Mrs. Vancouver, who was a kind-
hearted woman, and took a great interest
in her daughter's literary career, told me if
I could successfully carry out anything of
the kind, I might do so.   She did not in-
quire into particulars, nor did I explain them
to Miss Bessie ; but I told the latter that we
would not go out together into the garden,
but I would go first, and she should join me

about ten minutes afterward on the tower; out she was not to come if she saw any one about.

Near the top of the hill, above the garden, once stood an ancient mansion, of which nothing now remained but the remnants of some massive masonry. A courtyard, however, of this old edifice was still surrounded by a high wall, which formed the upper boundary of our garden. From a point near the tower a flight of twisting stone steps, flanked by blank walls, which turned themselves in various directions to suit the angles of the stairway, led to a green door in this wall. Through this door Miss Vancouver and myself, and doubtless many other persons, had often wished to pass; but it was locked, and, on inquiry, we found that there was no key to be had. The day previous, however, when wandering by myself, I had examined this door, and found that it was fastened merely by a snap-lock which had no handle, but was opened by a key. I had a knife with a long, strong blade, and pushing this into the hasp, I easily forced back the bolt. I then opened the door and walked into the old courtyard.

When Miss Vancouver appeared on the tower, I was standing at the top of the stone steps just mentioned, with the green door slightly ajar. Calling to her in a low tone, she ran up the steps, and, to her amazement, I ushered her into the court-yard and closed the door behind us.

"There," I exultingly exclaimed, "is our study, where we can write our story without interruption. We will come and go away separately; the people of the *pension* will not know that we are here or have been here, and there will be no occasion for that impertinent attention to which your mother so properly objects."

Miss Vancouver was delighted, and we walked about and surveyed the courtyard with much satisfaction. I had already selected the spot for our work. It was in the shade of an olive-tree, the only tree in the enclosure, beneath which there was a rude seat. I spread a rug upon the grass, and Miss Bessie sat upon the seat, and put her feet upon the rug, leaving room for me to sit thereon. We now took out our little blank-books and our stylograph pens and were ready for work. I explained that I had done nothing the day before, and Miss Vancouver said that had also been the case with her. She had not wished to do any-thing important without consultation; but

supposing that, of course, the hero was to
fall in love with the heroine, she thought
she might as well make him begin, but she
found she could not do it as she wished.
She wanted him to indicate to the lady that
he was in love with her without exactly
saying so. Could I not suggest some good
form for giving expression to this state of
things? After a little reflection, I thought
I could.

"I will speak," said I, "as if I were the
hero, and then you can see how it will
suit."

. "Yes," said she, "but you must not
forget that what you say should be very
gradual."

I tried to be as gradual as I could, and to
indicate by slow degrees the state of mind
in which we wished our hero to be. As the
indication became stronger and stronger, I
thought it right to take Miss Vancouver's
hand ; but to this she objected, because, as
she said, it was more than indication, and
besides, it prevented her from writing down
what I said. We argued this point a little
while without altering our position, and I
asserted that the hand-holding only gave
point and earnestness to the hero's remarks,
which otherwise would not be so natural

and true to life ; and if she wanted to use her right hand, her left hand would do to hold. We made this change, and I proceeded with the hero's remarks.

There was in our *pension* a young German girl named Margarita. She was a handsome, plump maiden, and spoke English very well. There was another young lady, also a German, named Gretzel. She was a little creature, and the fast friend of Margarita. These two had a companion whose name I did not know. She was a little older than the others, and was, I think, a Pole. She also understood English. As I was warming up toward the peroration of our hero's indication, I raised my eyes, and saw, on the brow of the hill, not a stone's-throw from us, these three girls. They were talking earnestly and walking directly toward us. The place where they were was used as a public pleasure-ground, and was separated from the old courtyard by a pale-fence. Although the girls could not come to us, there was nothing to prevent their seeing us if they chose to look our way, for they were on ground which was higher than the top of the fence.

When I saw these girls, I was horror-stricken, and my knees, on which I rested, trembled beneath me. I did not dare to rise, nor to change my position, for fear the motion should attract attention ; nor did I cease my remarks, for had I suddenly done so, my companion would have looked around to see what was the matter, and would certainly have jumped up, or have done something which would have brought the eyes of those girls upon us ; but my voice dropped very low, and I wondered if there was any way of my gently rolling out of sight.

But at this moment our young man with a mystery suddenly appeared on the other side of the fence, walking rapidly toward the girls. There was something on the ocean, probably a ship, to which he directed their attention ; and then he actually led them off, pointing, as it appeared, to a spot from which the distant object could be more plainly seen. They all walked away and disappeared behind the brow of the hill. With a great feeling of relief, I arose and recounted what had happened. Miss Vancouver sprang to her feet, shut up her blank-book, and put the stopper on her stylograph.

"This place will not do at all to work in," she said. "I will not have those girls staring at us."

I was obliged to admit that this particular spot would not do. I had not thought of any one walking in the grounds immediately above us, especially in the morning, which was our working time.

"They may return," she said, "and we must go away immediately and separately."

But I could not agree thus to give up our new-found study. The enclosure was quite extensive, with ruins at the other end, near which we might find some spot entirely protected from observation. So I went to look for such a place, leaving Miss Vancouver under the olive-tree, where, if she were seen alone, it would not matter. I found a spot which might answer, and, returning to the tree, sent her to look at it. While we were thus engaged, we heard the report of the noon cannon. This startled us both. The hour for *déjeûner à la fourchette* at the *pension* was twelve o'clock, and people were generally very prompt at that meal. It would not do for us to be late. Snatching up our effects, we hurried to the green door, but when I tried to open it as before, I found it impossible—a projecting strip of wood on the inside of the doorway preventing my reaching the bolt with my knife-blade. I tried to tear away the strip, but it was too firmly fastened. We both became very nervous and troubled. It was impossible to get out of the enclosure except through that door, for the wall was quite high and the top covered with broken glass embedded in the mortar. The party on the hill had had time to go down and around through the town to the *pension*. Our places at the table would be the only ones empty. What could attract more attention than this? And what would Mrs. Vancouver think and say? At this moment we heard some one working at the lock on the other side. The door opened, and there stood our hero.

"I heard some one at this door," he said ; "and supposing it had been accidentally closed, I came up and opened it."

"Thank you ; thank you very much !" cried Miss Vancouver.

And away she ran to the house. If only I were late, it did not matter at all. I followed with our hero, and endeavoured to make some explanation of the predicament of myself and the young lady. He took it all as a matter of course, as if the old court-yard were a place of general resort.

"When persons stroll through that door," he said, "they should put a piece of stick or of stone against the jamb, so that if the door is blown shut by the wind the latch may not catch."

And then he called my attention to a beautiful plant of the aloe kind which had just begun to blossom.

Miss Vancouver reached the breakfast-table in good time, but she told me afterward she would work in the old courtyard no more. The perils were too many.

For some days after this our story made little progress, for opportunities for consultation did not occur. I was particularly sorry for this, because I wanted very much to know how Miss Vancouver liked my indicative speech and what she had made of it. Early one afternoon about this time our hero, between whom and myself a slight acquaintance had sprung up, came to me and said—

" The sea is so perfectly smooth and quiet to-day that I thought it would be pleasant to take a row, and I have hired a boat. How would you like to go with me?"

I was pleased with his friendly proposition, and I am very fond of rowing; but yet I hesitated about accepting the invitation, for I hoped that afternoon to find some opportunity for consultation in regard to the work on which I was engaged.

"The boat is rather large for two persons," he remarked. "Have you any friends you would like to ask to go with us?"

This put a different phase upon affairs. I instantly said that I thought a row would be charming that afternoon, and suggested that Mrs. Vancouver and her daughter might like to take advantage of the opportunity.

The ladies were quite willing to go, and in twenty minutes we set off, two fishermen in red liberty caps pushing us from the pebbly beach. Our hero took one oar and I another, and we pulled together very well. The ladies sat in the stern, and enjoyed the smooth sea and the lovely day. We rowed across the little bay and around a high promontory, where there was a larger bay with a small town in the distance. The hero suggested that we should land here, as we could get some good views from the rocks. To this we all agreed; and when we had climbed up a little distance, Mrs. Vancouver found some wild-flowers which interested her very much. She was, in a certain way, a floraphobist, and took an especial delight in finding in foreign countries blossoms which were the same as or similar to flowers she was familiar with in New England.

Our hero had also a fancy for wild-flowers, and it was not long before he showed Mrs. Vancouver a little blossom which she was very sure she had seen either at East Gresham or Milton Centre. Leaving these two to their floral researches, Miss Vancouver and I climbed higher up the rocks, where the view would be better. We found a pleasant ledge ; and although we could not see what was going on below us, and the view was quite cut off in the direction of the town, we had an admirable outlook over the sea, on which, in the far distance, we could see the sails of a little vessel.

"This will be an admirable place to do a little work on our story," I said. "I have brought my blank-book and stylograph."

"And so have I," said she.

I then told her that I had been thinking over the matter a good deal, and that I believed in a short story two long speeches would be enough for the hero to make, and proposed that we should now go on with the second one. She thought well of that, and took a seat upon a rocky projection, while I sat upon another quite near.

"This second speech," said I, "ought to be more than indicative, and should express the definite purpose of the hero's sentiments; and I think there should be corresponding expressions from the heroine, and would be glad to have you suggest such as you think she would make." I then began to say what I thought a hero ought to say under the circumstances. I soon warmed up to my task wonderfully, and expressed with much earnestness and ardour the sentiments I thought proper for the occasion. I first held one of Miss Vancouver's hands, and then both of them, she trusting to her memory in regard to memoranda. Her remarks in the character of the heroine were, however, much briefer than mine, but they were enough. If necessary, they could be worked up and amplified. I think we had said all or nearly all there was to say when we heard a shout from below. It was our hero calling us. We could not see him, but I knew his voice. He shouted again, and then I arose from the rock on which Bessie was sitting and answered him. He now made his appearance some distance below us, and said that Mrs. Vancouver did not care to come up any higher to get the views, and that she thought it would be better to reach home before the sun should set.

That evening, in the *salon*, Bessie spoke

to me apart. "Our hero," she said, "is more than a hero; he is a guardian angel. You must fathom his mystery. I am sure that it is far better than anything we can invent for him."

I set myself to work to discover, if possible, not only the mystery which had first interested us in our hero, but also the reason and purpose of his guardian-angelship. He was an American, and now that I had come to know him better, I found him a very agreeable talker.

II.

Our hero was the first person whom I told of my engagement to Bessie. Mrs. Vancouver was very particular that this state of affairs should be made known. "If you are engaged," she said, "of course you can be together as much as you please. It is the custom in America, and nobody need make any remarks."

In talking to our hero, I told him of a good many little things that had happened at various times, and endeavoured by these friendly confidences to make him speak of his own affairs. It must not be supposed that I was actuated by prying curiosity, but certainly I had a right to know something of a person to whom I had told so much; but he always seemed a great deal more interested in us than in himself, and I took so much interest in his interest, which was very kindly expressed, that his affairs never came into our conversation.

But just as he was going away,—he left

the little town a few days before we did,—
he told me that he was a writer, and that
for some time past he had been engaged
upon a story,

Our story was never finished.   His was.
This is it.

THE END.